Stories

Shalom Auslander

SIMON & SCHUSTER PAPERBACKS

NEW YORK LONDON TORONTO SYDNEY

Simon & Schuster Paperbacks
Rockefeller Center
1230 Avenue of the Americas
New York, NY 10020

First Simon & Schuster paperback edition 2006

Simon & Schuster and colophon are registered
trademarks of Simon & Schuster, Inc.

For information regarding special discounts for bulk purchases,
please contact Simon & Schuster Special Sales:
1-800-456-6798 or business@simonandschuster.com

Designed by Karolina Harris
Title and half title art © Shepard Fairey and Studio Number One

Manufactured in the United States of America
10 9 8 7 6 5 4 3 2 1

The Library of Congress has catalogued the hardcover edition as follows:
Auslander, Shalom.
Beware of God: stories/Shalom Auslander.
p. cm.
1. Jews—Fiction. 2. Jewish fiction. I. Title.
PS3601 .U85 B49 2005
813'.6—dc22   2004051352

ISBN-13: 978-0-7432-6456-3
ISBN-10:   0-7432-6456-8
ISBN-13: 978-0-7432-6457-0 (Pbk)
ISBN-10:   0-7432-6457-6 (Pbk)

For Orli

I for one am going to take an heroic dose of magic mushrooms with my friends and head for the woods, where the word of God can be heard quite effortlessly and quite clearly without all the thees and thous. Hopefully, just before we leave, we'll catch a shot of the Pope bouncing around in his little Popemobile on the news. That'll give us something to giggle about for the first forty minutes before God starts speaking and we hush in silent reverie, and bask in his neverending, holy love.

—BILL HICKS

That sermons are preached in churches doesn't mean the churches don't need lightning conductors.

—GEORG CHRISTOPH LICHTENBERG

Contents

Contents

The War of the Bernsteins

THESE ARE THE THINGS that Bernstein carried in the brown, broken suitcase he kept under his bed in the hope that the Messiah would arrive in the middle of the night: two pairs of black socks, one pair of black pants, a white shirt, one Book of Psalms, some rugalach, three yarmulkes, a spare set of phylacteries, two prayer shawls (one for weekdays, one for Sabbath) and a bathing suit because you never know.

"In the World to Come," the rabbis would say to Bernstein, "there will be eternal happiness and joy."

"In the World to Come," Bernstein would say to his wife, "there will be eternal happiness and joy."

"I'm sorry you're so miserable here," Mrs. Bernstein replied from her post before the kitchen sink.

Bernstein lived every moment of this life in hopeful preparation for the next. Forty-five years of Torah study had convinced him not only of the sordidness of this world, but of the perfection and euphoria of the World to Come. As he got older, and that world steadily approached, Bernstein became ever more careful. Just last month, he had celebrated his fiftieth birthday.

"You're halfway to dead!" joked the birthday card Mrs. Bernstein had left for him. Mrs. Bernstein had a suitcase under her bed, too, but it wasn't packed for the Messiah.

Bernstein decided that with half his life already over, he was running out of time to score points. From now on, every action he took and every deed he considered would be put through a thorough cost/benefit analysis of reward versus punishment.

If he found himself to be too tired for morning services, he would remind himself of just how many rewards he'd receive in the World to Come if he could only get out of bed. He measured the lure of a one-time bacon double cheeseburger against the everlasting joy of love and peace. He weighed sitting in a buddy booth at the Show World Peep Center with an erection in his hand against sitting among the holy forefathers in the Garden of Eden with a crown of eternal love on his head.

The spiritual mathematics consumed him.

Was obeying a negative prohibition worth the same amount of reward in the World to Come as fulfilling a positive commandment? Would the inaction of negative prohibitions really be as rewarded as the deliberate action of positive commandments? If they were, could Bernstein simply not do those things that were negatively prohibited in this world and still be rewarded handsomely in the next, rather than actively doing those things that were positively commanded only to receive pretty much the same reward in the World to Come as if he had simply not done that which had been negatively prohibited? Would he actually be rewarded for not doing something, or would he just not receive the punishment he would have received if he had violated the negative prohibition? Then again, if the commandment was positive and he would receive punishment for not doing it, then would he receive rewards for doing it? Or was it just the not doing it that God was concerned with?

It gave Bernstein a terrible headache.

Mrs. Bernstein was only thirty-four years old last May, and was thus far more concerned with her lot in this world than with her lot in what was, in her own estimation, a decidedly dubious next.

"Let's go to the movies," Mrs. Bernstein said one boring Sunday afternoon.

Bernstein thought of all the cursing and immorality and nudity he might witness on the big screen, and how much euphoria in the World to Come it would cost him. *Your nakedness will be exposed and your shame uncovered. I will take vengeance; I will spare no one.*

"Nah," said Bernstein.

He briefly wondered if by renting *The Ten Commandments* he could be said to have fulfilled the commandment to *fill your heart and mind with Torah all the day and all the night.*

"Well, if we're staying home anyway," Mrs. Bernstein said, "let's make love." She grabbed him playfully around his waist. "Right here," she said, "in the kitchen!" Bernstein thought about how many rules of modesty that would cause him to violate, and how much ecstasy in the World to Come it could possibly cost him. *And the Lord said, because the cry of Sodom and Gomorrah is great, and because their sin is very grievous.*

"I'm tired," Bernstein said.

Mrs. Bernstein decided that if Bernstein thought she was going to waste her life securing his front-row seat in the afterlife, he had another thing coming. And it wasn't euphoria.

She decided to fight blessings with curses, piety with profanity. For every commandment, there was a prohibition. For every reward, there was a punishment. For every *mitzvah*, there was an equal and opposite *aveyrah*.

She bought a red silk nightie at Victoria's Secret and wore it casually around the house. She would cause him two sinful thoughts for every pious one in his thoughtless little head.

She bought jeans.

He spilled his semen on the ground. . . . What he did was wicked in the Lord's sight, so He put him to death.

The spiritual mathematics consumed her.

On the outside chance that there actually was a World to Come, she certainly didn't want to sacrifice her own rewards in the next life just to ruin his. Mrs. Bernstein didn't mind going to the Seventh Level of Hell, so long as she could walk to the edge, look down below and see Mr. Bernstein burning in the Eighth.

Sin selection became critical: she had to make sure that nothing she was doing to cause him to sin was actually costing her more points than his resultant sin would end up costing him—committing murder, for instance, just to get him to turn on the light on Shabbos. A felony, if you will, just to cause a misdemeanor. But what if the punishment for causing a sin was not only the punishment for the sin of causing someone to sin, but was also the punishment for the sin of whatever sin she caused? That is, would conspiracy to cause masturbation see her charged with both conspiracy and masturbation? Of course, if the total punishment of causing a sin is a sin of causation plus the sin of the sin that is being caused, then shouldn't causing a commandment to be fulfilled result in both the reward for the commandment of causing a positive commandment to be fulfilled plus the reward for the positive commandment she was causing to be fulfilled?

It gave her a terrible headache.

Bernstein began attending prayer services more frequently, praying more fervently, believing more believingly.

Fearing more fearfully.

He walked the mile and a half to synagogue for every Friday night service, every Saturday morning service, every Saturday afternoon service and every Saturday evening service. He attended weekday morning services every weekday morning, and weekday evening services every weekday evening.

He became president of the synagogue.

Blessed is he who helps in the construction of a synagogue.

She used nonkosher wine for Kiddush. She put milk in his coffee after serving him meat. She put pork in the chulent. She put bacon bits in his salad, and told him they were imitation.

"Those who eat the flesh of pigs and rats and other abominable things, they will meet their end together," declares the Lord.

He hung a large framed picture of the Lubavitcher Rebbe in his living room, which Mrs. Bernstein moved to the basement, which Bernstein moved back into the dining room.

Blessed is he who surrounds himself with the righteous.

(Bernstein figured he got himself a double-word score on that one, as he had *surrounded himself with the righteous* twice with just one picture.)

She set the alarm clock for Saturday morning. In his foggy half-sleep he would reach over and shut it off. Bam, Fourth Commandment.

Anyone who desecrates the Sabbath must surely be put to death.

The fool. He'd have to hang a hundred rabbi pictures around the house just to break even!

Bernstein began slaughtering his own chickens because he didn't trust his butcher.

He began cooking his own food because he didn't trust his wife.

He wore his tsitsit out, his beard long and his peyis curly. He purchased a black, wide-brimmed fur-felt Italian handmade Borsalino hat, for which he laid out a cool $365.

Blessed is he who spends his money on fulfilling God's commandments.

Mrs. Bernstein didn't buy herself a new hat. She wore the same frayed beret to synagogue that she'd worn for years.

They rarely spoke—even in the few odd moments when Bernstein wasn't at synagogue, doing charity work, praying or studying the Talmudic intricacies of who is liable to pay for damages if one man's bull gores another's (it depends who owns the field).

They lived opposite lives in opposite worlds.

One Friday night, after singing the grace after meals and reading the parsha of the week and saying the Shema Before Bedtime and kissing his tzitzit and touching them to his eyes and kissing them again and saying the Prayer Upon Sleeping and climbing into bed, Bernstein rolled over and tapped his wife on her shoulder.

"Blessed is he who obeys God's command to be fruitful and multiply," he whispered gently in her ear.

Mrs. Bernstein stared silently at the doorway. "I want a divorce," she finally said.

There was a long silence.

Mrs. Bernstein sat up and swung her legs over the side of the bed.

" 'I hate divorce,' says the Lord God of Israel," threatened Bernstein. *"So guard yourself in your spirit, and do not break faith!"*

Beneath her robe Mrs. Bernstein wore her pink sweater set and white Reeboks. She stood up, let the robe drop from her shoulders and picked up her car keys.

"The husband will be innocent of any wrongdoing!" shouted Bernstein. *"But the woman will bear the consequences of her sin!"*

These are the things Mrs. Bernstein carried in the tan leather valise she kept under her bed in the hope she would someday find the courage to leave her husband in the middle of the night: two pairs of black tights, the red silk nightie, her jeans, a makeup bag, a pack of cigarettes, the spring fashion issue of *Vogue* and a bathing suit.

Because you never know.

Bobo the Self-Hating Chimp

AT 9:37 in the otherwise ordinary morning of May 25, Bobo, a small male chimpanzee in the Monkey House of the Bronx Zoo, achieved total conscious self-awareness.

God.

Death.

Shame.

Guilt.

Each one dropped like a boulder onto his tiny primitive skull. He grabbed his head in his hands and ran shrieking around the Monkey House, overturning the water bowls and tearing branches off the trees. He threw himself to the ground, kicking and screaming. He grabbed a fallen branch and began chasing the smaller chimps around the old oak tree.

Suddenly he froze. Bobo closed his eyes and leaned against the tree for support. It was as if he had been somehow transported to the top of the tallest tree in the forest and was looking down upon himself below. Bobo saw a brute, a beast, a dim, half-finished creature using his newly acquired skills not to build or to better, but to brandish a weapon. He also noticed he was sporting a bright red erection. Shame filled his soul.

Shame?

That was new.

The children who were gathered around Bobo's cage began to scream and cry, tears streaming down their faces. Horrified elfin jurors, they pointed their little fingers at Bobo's hideous primate penis.

The mortified teachers skipped right over Explanation and went straight to Denial.

"He's just happy, children!" tried one teacher.

"Happy, yay!" clapped the other.

They quickly led the little innocents outside. Management had no choice. The Monkey House was closed for the day, and Bobo was sedated.

The Monkey House is located a short walk away

from the last Skyfari stop, just across the way from the World of Reptiles. For the past year and a half there had been the constant hammering, sawing and diesel-engine-starting of facility improvements. RV parking had been added near Wild Asia, and they had spruced up the water fountain outside Giraffe World with real Mexican tiles. Administration East got new computers.

The Monkey House restoration was the most recent, and most elaborate, of them all. Those monkeys made their numbers. "They pull in the crowds," said management.

Renovations began in early March in order to be finished in time for the Memorial Day rush. The chain link fences were gone, replaced by clear, high-tensile-strength glass. The first week many of the chimps smashed into the glass midswing, but soon learned. Gone, too, was the drab decor, replaced with exotic white birch trees, maple trees, an even grander, older oak and the crown jewel of the empire, Chimpanzee Bay, a freshwater pool that was built to look like an ocean, complete with a Deluxe WaveMaker 3000. Judging by the crowds pressing their faces to the glass on opening day, it didn't seem to bother anyone that chimpanzees can't actually swim.

The humans outside the glass all seemed quite pleased with themselves, but for the lesser primates inside, the renovations caused nothing but anxiety. Beebee, Shirley, Topo and Sweetface were all on antidepressants, Ladybird had mysteriously stopped menstruating and Koko had to be sent to a small animal farm in Northern New Jersey for recuperation. The doctors expected this.

"We expected this," they said.

And so, when Bobo made the same astonishing evolutionary leap as our primate ancestors made so very long ago, the doctors quickly misdiagnosed it as posttraumatic stress disorder, discontinued his Viagra, and scripted him for a month of Paxil, five milligrams a day.

Bobo awoke some time later to find himself in a small steel box. His head felt heavy. The front wall of the box was a metal grid, through which Bobo could see many similar boxes across the way.

He wanted out.

A lab technician at the far end of the room was enjoying her morning feeding and a cup of coffee as she read the *New York Post*. He would appeal to her humanity. "You and I are indeed different," he would say. "But surely the awareness of our own mortality and the unique self-perception we share more than compensate for the fraction of a fraction of a difference in our physical genetic makeup."

Bobo's mind may have evolved, but his larynx had not. And so, in place of an impassioned plea for understanding, he grabbed the cage with both hands and legs and shrieked as loudly as he could.

Bobo was sedated.

The next morning, the zookeepers decided to see if Bobo could be safely reintroduced to the Monkey House. Bobo was no fool; he knew what they wanted. They wanted Curious George. They wanted Megillah Gorilla. They wanted Monchichi.

They wanted Monkey.

Bobo held the vet's hand as she walked him back inside the house. They loved it when he did that. Elbows high, hands scratching his armpits, Bobo did an exaggerated chimp walk over to the food bin and peeled a bright yellow banana.

"Ooo ooo ooo! Ah ah ah!"

The zookeepers smiled, nodded and wrote on their clipboards.

Bobo walked back and forth, scratched his ass and rubbed his crotch. He swung from a low birch branch. "Ooo ooo ooo! Ah ah ah!"

The zookeepers smiled, nodded and wrote on their clipboards.

He sat down next to a female chimp named Esmeralda. Esmeralda stood up and bent over. Bobo mounted her.

The zookeepers smiled, nodded and wrote on their clipboards.

"I'm sorry," Bobo said to Esmeralda when the zookeepers had gone. "That was wrong of me." He sat down and sighed heavily. Esmeralda moved behind him and began picking the bugs from his hair.

"I know you probably don't understand the concept of right and wrong," said Bobo, "at least not in the Judeo-Christian sense of the words. I didn't myself until just recently. Still, I used you. Selfishly. I objectified you. And for what? To save my own hide? Or perhaps still worse, out of some violent animus, some stubborn genetic trait of survivalism that even nature can't filter out? Damn all my high philosophies! I deserve to be locked in this cage with you monkeys."

Esmeralda pulled a yellow-winged bug from Bobo's shoulder, examined it closely for a moment and stuck it in her mouth. She stood up, brushed herself off and walked away.

"Wait!" called Bobo.

There was something about this Esmeralda, something in her eyes. Maybe she was different. Bobo wondered if they could someday leave this zoo together, get a place nearby in Rye, maybe Larchmont, something with a fence and a swing set for the kids.

Bobo scrambled after her but he was too late. Esmeralda swung from tree to tree, straight across to the far end of the Monkey House where Mongo, one of the house's larger males, was closely examining his scrotum. Esmeralda nudged Mongo, turned her back to him and bent over with all the ceremony of someone who'd just dropped a quarter. Mongo mounted her.

Bobo instantly loathed her. Then he immediately regretted loathing her.

Regret?

That was new.

Bobo watched with contempt as Mongo humped away at Esmeralda, his ridiculous testicles bouncing this way and that like terrified children on the back of a runaway camel in the African Safari park. "Help!" they seemed to shout. "Get us out of here!"

Bobo knew how they felt. Look at us, Bobo

thought, shaking his head sadly. A bunch of fucking monkeys. Where is our dignity? Where is our pride? Where are our pants?

Mongo finished with Esmeralda, walked over to where Bobo was sitting and shat.

A typical leader.

Bobo could not believe the amount of shit in this tiny chimpanzee world. There was shit on the floor, shit in the cave, shit by the sunflowers. There was shit in the water bowls, and shit on the jungle gym.

As Mongo lumbered back to his bed on the far side of the cage, Bobo grabbed a handful of Mongo's shit and threw it at him as best he could. Bobo didn't have much of a pitching arm, or opposable thumbs, and the turd sailed sloppily past Mongo and landed with a wet thud on the wall just beyond him. It held there for a moment, and Bobo scratched his head.

"Huh," Bobo thought. "Kinda looks like a chimp."

And with that, Bobo scooped up another handful of shit, walked over to the glass and began to paint.

By the end of his first week of consciousness, Bobo had painted large Expressionistic shit murals on every wall of the Monkey House. He began with simple studies: an apple, a monorail, cotton candy. By the end of the first week, he was creating sweeping tableaus which he saw as scathingly satirical attacks on chimpanzee culture and primate mores. His *Self-Portrait* was a devastating attack on racism, his *Unhuman Stain* a poignant plea for self-respect and dignity, his *Life in the Monkey House* a searing assault on political power and corporate gain.

Bobo's paintings not only exhibited true artistic promise, they were—at $35,000 a pop—a much-needed additional revenue stream for the zoo. Management gently steered him toward Werthmeyer oil paints and hand-stretched canvases (they had, after all, spent almost $3 million on those glass walls). They even splurged for a mahogany easel with height adjustment and bonus stow-away paint tray.

This wasn't nearly as therapeutic for Bobo as it may have appeared. He was tortured. His mind was expanding at a phenomenal rate. All he could see was the shit around him, and all the paint in the world could never cover it up.

His paintings grew darker with every passing day. Reds became blues, greens became blacks. While the humans took snapshots, Bobo wrestled with existence and meaning and death.

And Esmeralda.

Of course she would prefer Mongo over him!

Why not? It was a mutually selfish relationship; he only wanted to fuck, she only wanted to breed. They were perfect for each other!

Let them, he thought.

Let them sniff and poke and prod, let them debase themselves and all chimpkind.

Bobo was spending much of his time alone, curled up in the darkest corner he could find. "Aww," said the tourists tapping loudly on the glass, "you're an angry little monkey, aren't you? Yes, you are!"

He stopped painting. Management optimistically distributed Bobo's art supplies to the rest of the chimps, albeit with little success: Mongo tore apart the canvases to make himself a bed, and Esmeralda had to be hospitalized after eating a half dozen tubes of Cadmium Yellow. Her skin tone was never the same again.

On June 12, just two weeks after he first gained consciousness, Bobo stood up and walked calmly to the edge of Chimpanzee Bay.

He put one foot in, then the other. The humans waved and smiled. Bobo walked further into the water, one step after another.

He didn't struggle or flail.

He made no attempt to swim.

Bobo stayed below the waves for some time. The

rest of the chimps stood by and watched with anx-
ioius curiosity.

Esmeralda bent over.

Mongo mounted her.

After some time, Bobo's body bobbed gently up
to the surface. The Wavemaker 3000 nudged it slowly
back to shore.

A small chimp named Kato stood on a large, flat
quarry stone that extended out into the Bay.

God.

Death.

Shame.

Guilt.

Each one dropped like a boulder onto his tiny
primitive skull. He grabbed his head in his hands and
shrieked. All of a sudden, it was as if Kato had been
somehow transported to the top of the tallest tree in
the forest, and was looking down upon himself
below. Kato saw a group of God's first drafts sitting
complacently by as one of their own took his life,
not only unable to offer any assistance but unable
even to relate, to understand, to get beyond bananas
and shit and Esmeralda's vagina.

"Look at us," Kato thought. "A bunch of fucking
monkeys."

He grabbed a long, bare branch from the Monkey House floor and used it to gently pull Bobo's body back to shore.

Nobody else seemed to mourn. No one else seemed to feel. Shame filled Kato's soul.

Shame?

That was new.

Somebody Up There Likes You

Bloom's Volvo finally came to rest upside down on the right-hand shoulder of the New York State Thruway. The roof was collapsed, the front end was crushed, and the driver's side door was torn nearly in half.

The policeman shook his head.

"You're very lucky."

Bloom nodded.

"Somebody up there likes you."

Bloom nodded.

Whatever dying mechanism was coughing black smoke from the underside of the car soon ignited. The car filled with flames, incinerating Bloom's insurance papers, his registration, the picture of his deceased grandparents that hung from his rearview mirror and his Coach Executive briefcase, which contained the 300-page report on emerging Asian markets he'd promised to have in by Monday morning and the only copy of a screenplay he'd been secretly working on. It was a romantic comedy.

The fireman shook his head.

"You're very lucky."

Bloom nodded.

"Saved by an angel."

Bloom nodded.

Sirens screamed, radios crackled.

Bloom was leaning against the guardrail, trying to catch his breath, when from some dark, dusty distant part of his mind, some cobwebbed corner of forgotten phylacteries and skullcaps, came words Bloom hadn't said or heard or even thought in the past thirty years:

Shema Yisroel Adonai Eloheinu Adonai Echad

F UCK," said God.

The angels stood quietly at the back of His office,

their eyes locked nervously on the place where their feet would have been. The Angel of Death—the bearer of the afternoon's cosmically bad news—wrung his hands nervously as he stood before God's enormous oak desk. Lucifer stood behind God, calmly cleaning his gun.

"What do you mean he walked away from it?" asked God.

Death shrugged. "I don't know, Boss. Not a scratch on him."

The angels sang, their sweet, melodic voices ascending as one. "Hallelu . . ."

"Not now," said God.

He closed His eyes and massaged His temples, trying to stave off the migraine He knew was coming. He was getting tired of this. Tired of the whole damn business.

Heaven fell silent, from the Pearly Gates out front to the steel service door out back. You could practically hear Hell.

"Something about side impact protection or something," offered Death.

"What was he driving?" asked Lucifer. "Volvo or some shit, right?"

"S40 sedan," said Death.

Lucifer nudged God. "See? What'd I tell you about those things? Pain in the ass."

"Hummers are even worse," said Death.

"Yeah, but at least you can flip a Hummer," said Lucifer.

"I've flipped plenty of Hummers," said Death, "don't tell me about flipping Hummers. Flipping a Hummer isn't good for killing anybody."

"Are you telling me that flipping a Hummer isn't going to injure the driver?"

"It's not a question of injuring," said Death, "it's a question of *critically* injuring."

"But you could definitely flip a Hummer, that's my point."

"Enough," said God. "Enough." They never seemed to tire of it.

He pulled open the top drawer of his desk, took out his handgun, and shoved a few cartridges into his pocket.

"Lucifer," He said. "Get the car."

The angels sang, their sweet, melodic voices ascending up as one. "Hallelu . . ."

"Not now," said God.

...

THE question troubled Bloom deeply. Did somebody up there like him, as the rescue workers had suggested, or did somebody up there dislike him? Was somebody up there trying to save him, or was somebody up there trying to kill him?

Was it a miracle, or was it a warning?

And didn't anybody up there like Luis Soto, the drunk driver they'd just dragged off the bloody hood of Bloom's car?

Surely, Bloom reasoned, if God wanted to kill him, God could kill him. Then again, if God wanted him dead, why the Volvo? If death is predetermined, wouldn't automobile purchases be predetermined? Didn't the Volvo—the prudence, the zero percent financing—didn't they all collectively prove that someone up there liked Bloom?

On the other hand, it was possible that God had been trying to kill Bloom—that nobody up there liked Bloom and that something had simply gone wrong. It was a big operation, there were bound to be some mistakes. Sometimes Bloom sent Amanda out for a cappuccino and she came back with a latte.

It happens. A file misfiled. A printer misprinting. A celestial goof. A Jehovian cock-up.

The cab came to a stop outside his apartment building. "Eighteen dollars even," said the driver.

Eighteen, thought Bloom. The numerical value of the Hebrew word for "life." He was eschatologically spiraling. Bloom paid the driver, went inside and phoned his mother.

LUCIFER floored it until they reached Manhattan, but even for archangels, crosstown traffic on a Friday evening was treacherously slow-going.

God stared sullenly out the passenger side window. He hated coming down here.

"What a dump," he thought.

This micromanaging bullshit depressed him. Fucking Bloom. Scheduled for death over six months ago, the guy was still strolling around the Upper West Side of Manhattan. It was supposed to have been a simple mugging, nothing fancy: Bloom gets on a downtown train, some kid pulls a knife, Bloom gets it in the stomach. Death pulled off a thousand of those things a week. But that day, of all days, Bloom oversleeps. Late for his appointment, he runs outside and instead of taking the train, he jumps in a cab.

One botched death, and there was no end of problems. Bloom's death had taken months to reschedule, and now it had gone wrong once again.

"Defibrillators," Lucifer was saying. "That's the problem. Before defibrillators, keeping on schedule was a piece of cake."

"It's not the defibrillators," said Death. "It's the multinational pharmaceutical industry."

"Sure, the multinational pharmaceutical industry," said Lucifer. "But without defibrillators, there wouldn't be any need for the multinational pharmaceutical industry, that's all I'm saying."

"What about CPR?"

"CPR? Please. I'd take CPR over defibrillators any day."

God lit a cigarette and rolled down His window. People thought His job was easy. All their preposterous prayers, like He was some great big Fonzarelli in the sky, walking around, snapping His fingers and slapping jukeboxes.

Save me, heal me, cure me.

Like He could if He wanted to. They were all part of the same cosmic continuum, Himself included.

They couldn't even begin to appreciate the amount of work that went into just one single death. And not just human deaths: animal, plant, insect, alien, on all the planets in all the universes. And not just now, but in the past, the present, the future.

Creation was a production nightmare.

Could they ever in their limited minds conceive of the number of scheduling difficulties involved in getting just the right people, on just the right days, at just the right locations, death after death after death? It was an antemortem house of cards, one missed death upsetting the entire birth/death/birth cycle for every universe in every dimension. All those should-be-deads walking the Earth, saying things never meant to be said, to people never meant to be met, a catastrophic ripple effect through the story structure of an infinite number of lives after lives after lives.

And all the while, *"Heal us, O Lord, bring recovery for our ailments! For you are God, King, the faithful and compassionate healer!"*

Pains in the ass.

You should give a little charity," Bloom's mother was saying. "It's Shabbos tomorrow, would it kill you to have a Shabbos? Maybe go to shul tonight, give a little thanks?"

He hated the way she pushed religion on him. Like it was drugs. Like one hit off her crack pipe of belief and she'd hook him for life.

Now it seemed she'd been right all along.

All of them—his mother, his father, his rabbis, his friends—they'd all been right about God.

About His wrath, anyway.

"I'll go to shul," he promised his mother before putting down the phone. "I will."

Bloom hadn't been to a synagogue in years, didn't even know where the synagogue was.

What a fool he had been!

One day a week, was that too much for God to ask? God forbid he should miss a Yankee game, but an opportunity to do a mitzvah, that he could miss. Here he was, a member of a health club, a video club, a member of American Express. But was he a member of a synagogue? What a waste he had made of his life!

His life, that made him laugh.

His Volvo.

His doorman apartment.

His Prada shoes and his Rossignol skis.

His, his, his!

Would they save him from God's wrath? Could he bribe his way out of Gehenom with his Hugo Boss suit and his Mont Blanc pen?

"Don't anger Him," his mother had begged.

"Do what He says and nobody gets hurt," the rabbis had warned.

"Honk if you love God," the bumper sticker had urged.

But had Bloom ever honked? No. He hadn't honked once.

Bloom needed air.

And he needed a synagogue.

Wʜᴀᴛ about cancer?" asked Lucifer.

"Cancer was good for a while," said Death, "but now there's chemotherapy."

"Only with early detection."

"True" said Death. "But they're detecting it earlier and earlier."

"Listen," argued Lucifer, "you can't discount the entire time-honored concept of disease as an effective killer simply because some men—in First World countries only, mind you—are having their balls checked a few years earlier."

"I'm not discounting the entire concept of disease as an effective killer," said Death, "I'm just saying cancer's overrated."

"Oh, yes, well, I'll give you that," said Lucifer. "Tuberculosis. Now that was a disease."

Lately the should-be-deads were everywhere. Medication, heart transplants, chemotherapy, triple bypasses, MediVac, brain surgery. No amount of wars or disease, it seemed, could keep God on schedule.

He was just trying to keep the ball spinning. There were rules. There were regulations. People needed to be born, and people needed to die, and as passionately as they embraced the former they stubbornly resisted the latter.

"Don't blame me!" God wanted to shout from the top of the tallest mountain. Everest. K2. No Sinai bullshit this time. Don't blame me for the fires. Don't blame me for the floods, for the famines, for the plagues. Don't blame me.

I'm just doing my job.

I can't save you.

My hands are tied.

The car screeched to a stop in front of Bloom's building. God took out His gun, switched off the safety and tucked it inside His blazer.

"Let's get this over with," He said.

AND Abraham awoke in the morning, and he went forth.

Bloom didn't know how long he had been walking before he discovered the old synagogue. He wasn't
even sure what street he was on. But even after all
these years, he still recognized the ancient Hebrew
writing above the door: *Repentance, prayer and charity
remove the evil of His decree.*

After all this time, there was still some time.

Wasn't that the beauty of religion?

Wasn't that the majesty of Hashem?

A life like Bloom's, wasted on the material and the
superficial, redeemed with the simplest of actions—
repentance, prayer, a bit of charity. God in His Neverending Mercy asked nothing more than that.

Would your boss forgive you so easily?

Would your wife or girlfriend take you back so
readily after so many years of neglect?

It had been a long time since Bloom had been inside a synagogue. Over the years, he'd made sure to
avoid any places that even vaguely resembled one.
The New York Public Library, for instance, completely creeped him out. The gothic archways, the

high ceilings, row after row of old tattered books. Even the Metropolitan Museum of Art disturbed him. He could stomach the exhibitions, but he stayed well away from the bookstore.

He opened a dusty old prayer book, and turned to the evening service.

"Forgive us, our Father, for we have erred. Pardon us, our King, for we have willfully sinned."

A droplet fell onto the page before him, and Bloom realized that he was crying.

"Blessed are you, O Lord, the Gracious One who pardons abundantly."

FUCK," said God.

Bloom's apartment had been empty, and they were back in the car, heading across town.

"He could be anywhere," said Death.

"I hate this goddamn city," said Lucifer.

"Turn left here," said God.

God knew where Bloom was. He was where they all went when they wanted to make His job more difficult than it had to be.

"Right here," said God. "Pull over."

Bloom gently closed his prayer book, kissed the

cover and walked silently out to the lobby. He felt a new, keener sense of his place in the world, as if by sparing his body, God had reawakened his soul.

As Bloom pushed on the heavy synagogue door that led to the chaotic, Godless city beyond, he noticed a small shelf hanging humbly beside the doorway. The shelf was lined with a number of charity collection boxes—for children in Israel, for the poor, for the UJA.

Repentance, prayer and charity remove the evil of His decree.

Bloom reached into his pocket, and divided whatever money he had between them.

What was the value of money in the face of God's eternal judgment?

The night was warm and muggy, but Bloom felt more alive than he had in years. He smiled, put his hands in his pockets and headed across the street.

He heard the squeal of tires behind him, but there wasn't even time to turn around before the car slammed into his back, throwing him up in the air and into oncoming traffic. A taxicab coming the other way couldn't stop, and hit Bloom a second time before his body finally crumpled to the ground.

Death checked out the back window.

"Got him," he said.

Lucifer nodded.

"Got him."

*C*IGARETTES?" asked Lucifer. "You're going to tell me that *cigarettes* are a more efficient killer than tuberculosis?"

Death and Lucifer sat in God's office, playing poker and sharing a bottle of wine.

"It's not a question of efficiency," said Death, "it's a question of precision. You give one person TB, you give a thousand people TB. Then you spend the next hundred years rebirthing all the people who weren't supposed to die in the first place. You're just creating more work for yourself. I'm saying, you get your guy hooked on Camels, boom—you got yourself one dead guy. No fuss, no muss."

"Yeah, but what about secondhand smoke?"

"You're comparing a couple of accidental kills off secondhand smoke to a viral plague that wiped out half of Europe?"

"If you're talking accuracy," said Lucifer, "I'll give

you cigarettes over tuberculosis. But efficiency-wise—I'm talking bang for the buck—TB wins hands down. That's my point."

Death looked around.

"Where's God, anyway?" he asked.

"At the funeral," said Lucifer.

"He still goes to those?" asked Death.

Lucifer shrugged. "Full house," he said, laying down his cards.

"Damn."

Fuck," said God.

The angels stood quietly at the back of the cemetery, their eyes locked nervously on the place where their feet would have been.

As Bloom's body was lowered into the grave, the rabbi stood and prayed aloud:

"The Rock! Perfect in every way. Who can say to Him, "What have you done?" He rules above and below, brings death and resuscitates, brings down to the grave and rises up! God gave and God took away, Blessed is the name of Hashem!"

The angels sang, their sweet, melodic voices ascending as one. "Hallelu . . ."

"Not now," said God.

Bloom's mother began to weep.

God closed his eyes and massaged His temples, trying to stave off the migraine He knew was coming. He was getting tired of this.

Tired of the whole damn business.

Heimish Knows All

IT was Shabbos morning, and Heimish lay un-easily on his tartan dogbed beside the radiator, watching Shlomo furiously jerking himself off. Heimish's dark, wet eyes filled with loathing and contempt.

"Look at you," the dog said. "If it weren't so sinful it'd be pathetic."

Shlomo was only ten years old and somewhat new to the whole masturbating thing, so he needed every bit of concentration he could muster.

"Ugh," growled Heimish, "have some self-respect."

Shlomo angrily stood up, held a towel in front of himself and opened the bedroom door.

"Whoa, whoa," said Heimish. "Watch where you're pointing that thing."

"Out!" said Shlomo. "Go on!"

"Oh, thank God," said Heimish as he slinked toward the door. "I thought you wanted to fuck me."

"Out!"

"Pig."

Shlomo slammed the door. What a pain in the ass that dog had been lately. He looked down at the shriveling organ in his hand.

"You call that a penis?" he thought to himself.

Shlomo felt ashamed. He worried that God would punish him. He had been told by his rabbis that if you masturbate you go to hell and they boil you in a pot filled with all the semen that you wasted in your lifetime. He wondered if the rabbis were right. He wondered how full his pot was.

He went back to bed, added a few more shots to his boiling cauldron and got dressed for shul.

THE first time Shlomo heard the term *blowjob*, he spent a week crouched over on the toilet, desperately blowing at his penis like a lost hiker trying to start a fire. Everything Shlomo learned about sex he had learned at third hand from his classmates who had learned it at second hand from their brothers who had learned it at first hand from their fathers' pornography. After nearly hyperventilating, he tried using his mother's hairdryer (both warm and cold settings), but with little success. His father had been waiting for him outside the bathroom door. "Faigaleh," he'd said angrily, and slapped Shlomo hard across his face. "Blow dryers are for girls."

The few semantic clues Shlomo managed to piece together only made the physical mystery that much greater.

Cock?

Snatch?

Twat?

What could a twat possibly be?

He was able to figure out that jerking off was something he could do to himself, but there was nothing in the language that offered any specific instruction. And then, just last week, Chaim Laifer referred to Rabbi Grunembaum as "a jerkoff" while vigorously pumping his fist up and down.

It was like discovering a secret handshake.

Not that it was easy. He tried a few times, but it tickled terribly and Shlomo would stop, afraid that any more secret handshaking would make him pee in his bed. But last night, after everyone had fallen asleep from the heavy Friday evening meal, Shlomo bravely decided to risk it.

He'd locked the bathroom door, gotten undressed and slipped into the bathtub with a bottle of his mother's Jergens. He figured that if he did pee, well, at least it would be in the bathtub.

Shlomo didn't pee.

A thick white fluid he'd never seen before came out of him and slid sadly down his tightly clenched fingers.

"Dear God," thought Shlomo. "What have I done?"

He felt like crying.

His sin was everywhere.

It was like trying to clear a murder scene. He mopped the murdered Jewish souls off his hands with a couple of tissues, flushed them down the toilet and hid the Jergens behind the medicine rack. Shlomo quickly dressed and opened the bathroom door, ready for the dash to his bedroom.

Heimish sat waiting outside the bathroom door.

"I hope you're happy," Heimish said to him. "You just flushed a million Jews down the toilet."

Shlomo stomped at Heimish, who yelped and ran away.

He lay awake for some time that night, staring at the ceiling through the darkness and wondering how God would punish him. He had been told by his rabbis that when you die, all the souls you murdered in each wasted ejaculation would gather together and chase you through the firmament, hounding you for eternity. He wondered if the rabbis were right. He wondered if Heimish was right. He buried a few million more souls in a Kleenex and fell asleep.

SHLOMO clipped on his tie and went downstairs for breakfast.

"Well, look who's here," said Heimish, looking up from his bowl of kibble. "Boy," Heimish said under his breath to Shlomo's mother, "I could tell you some stories."

"Get out of here!" Shlomo yelled at Heimish.

"What are you doing?" Shlomo's mother asked. "Heimish, stay. You're a good boy."

"One load last night, another this morning," said Heimish. "The kid's a machine."

"He's always watching me," grumbled Shlomo.

"He loves you," his mother said. "Have some breakfast."

"I'm late for shul."

It was a cool autumn morning. Shlomo buttoned his suit jacket and pulled his collar up around his neck. It was beginning to feel a lot like Yom Kippur.

Shlomo would have a lot of repenting to do that day.

He walked down the steep hill of Pine Road, and made the right turn onto Carlton Lane. As he passed by the Hirschs' mailbox, something at the edge of the woods caught his eye.

It was the fluttering page of an old magazine. But it wasn't the fluttering that caught his eye, it was the color of the page.

It was pink.

Pornography pink.

Shlomo checked both ways to see if anybody was watching, and ducked into the woods.

The magazine was called *Juggs*. He picked up the

magazine and walked a bit farther into the woods.

What Shlomo had discovered, according to the tagline, wasn't just any porno mag—it was The Dirtiest Tit Mag in the World. On the cover, a woman named Candy Cantaloupes licked a half-peeled banana which she held between her unfeasibly humongous breasts. Candy had recently been named the Slut of The Year, an award she certainly seemed to deserve. On page 23, Candy lay happily on her back while a man straddled her chest. He had put his penis where until then only bananas had been.

The very idea!

Shlomo's mind reeled.

Putting a penis between breasts! Who thought of such things! He started to stiffen. Shlomo unzipped his pants and began to rub himself.

Suddenly he heard the unmistakable sound of a twig snapping behind him. Shlomo jumped, tried to hide his nakedness and spun around to see who was . . .

Heimish.

Heimish wagged his tail and cocked his head curiously at both Shlomo and Shlomo's penis, which had, in all the excitement, made its way back out of his pants.

"What's the commotion?" his penis seemed to ask.

"Dear God," asked Heimish, "can't you go one hour without debasing yourself?"

Shlomo picked up a stick and threw it hard at Heimish. "Get out of here!" he spat at the whimpering hound. Heimish went back to the road and trotted back home with his head held low.

"You're sick, you know that!" called Heimish. "Sick!"

Shlomo stuffed the magazine inside his jacket sleeve and continued on his way to shul.

The congregation was already halfway through the service. Shlomo paused outside the doorway; he worried for a moment that if he walked inside he would burst into flames.

He held his breath and slowly reached for the doorknob. He turned it gently and pushed the door open.

Phew.

It was ten-thirty already, and the rabbi was most of the way through his sermon, so Shlomo decided to wait outside in the lobby with all the young mothers with their babies and their strollers and their tight, silk blouses you could see their lacy, pointy bras through.

Shlomo watched them from a safe perch high on the steps to the women's section. He loved seeing

women with babies. They may as well have been wearing a sign that read "I have sex." There was no denying it. Just knowing that he was surrounded with all these women who would put cocks in their twats drove Shlomo absolutely mad.

He ran to the men's room, found an empty stall and locked the door.

As Rabbi Teitelbaum finished his Shabbos speech on the power of davening, Shlomo ejaculated on Tiffany Mound's mounds.

He shoved the magazine back into his jacket. He knew that if he picked up a siddur now he would burst into flames. He turned the tap above the sink just as Dr. Kaplan walked in.

"Good Shabbos," said Dr. Kaplan as he started to pee.

"Good Shabbos," said Shlomo as he washed the sin off his hands. He looked out the window, and noticed a dog out there, calmly waiting at the end of the shul driveway.

Heimish.

Over the driveway, through the trees, past the main entrance, through the bathroom window, Heimish looked directly at Shlomo and shook his head in disgust.

That was all Shlomo needed, that damn dog blabbing to everyone.

"Great," said Heimish. "You've defiled a synagogue. Why don't you stop by the Holocaust Museum on the way home and defile that, too?"

A group of older boys walked over to Heimish and began to pet him.

"Hey, Heimish!" one said.

"What's shakin', Heimish," said another.

"Mmm," Heimish whispered to Shlomo. "It's so nice to be petted by hands unsullied by the sin of emission."

Shlomo pulled his suit jacket tightly around the dirtiest tit mag in the world and ran outside. He made his way as quickly as he could through the busy lobby, dodging the rabbi and strollers and toys.

"You know my owner, right?" Heimish was probably saying to the older boys, making the secret jerk-off motion with his paw. "Big time."

Shlomo ducked three dentists, an obstetrician and a lawyer before running face first into Mrs. Malinowitz's tremendous bosom. Mrs. Malinowitz was sixty-two years old and grossly overweight, but Shlomo couldn't resist pausing for just one split second to nuzzle gently between her pendulous breasts.

She smelled of gefilte fish and Chanel.

Shlomo knew most of Mrs. Malinowitz was plain old fat, but he didn't really care. Whatever percentage of the tits engulfing his face was fat, some of it was definitely genuine tit.

"He's probably jerking off right now," Heimish would be telling the boys. They'd all be laughing and high-fiving each other at Shlomo's expense.

"Tell your mother I said 'Good Shabbos,' " said Mrs. Malinowitz as Shlomo hurried through the heavy front door.

Heimish stood up and started wagging his tail. The older boys had already gone.

"Mrs. Malinowitz?" asked Heimish. "You've got to be kidding me! *Thou shalt not covet thy neighbor's wife!*"

Shlomo stomped furiously toward him.

"Get!" he said harshly. "Get! Go on!" Heimish didn't budge. Shlomo reached into his suit jacket, pulled out the magazine and rolled it tightly. He swung it at Heimish with all his might.

"Away!" he said.

Shlomo swung again.

Heimish ducked, his tail between his legs. Heimish

wasn't sure whether Shlomo was playing with him or not. Shlomo swung the magazine again, this time hitting Heimish squarely on his left haunch.

"Bad dog!" Shlomo shouted. "Go home!" Heimish knew he wasn't playing now. Shlomo raised the magazine above his head again, and Heimish darted into the busy street.

The driver of the car never saw him. She only stepped on the brakes after feeling a thump coming from under the left rear tire.

"Ohmigod!" she cried.

She had been on her way to the movies.

She was blond.

Her T-shirt said PORN STAR.

That night, Shlomo sat in bed with his knees drawn up to his chest, the *Juggs* magazine opened on the bed beside him. He missed Heimish, but he was glad to finally be alone with Kimberley Kupps and Wendy Whoppers and Nikki Knockers.

"You call that a penis?" Nikki said to him.

He felt ashamed.

He worried that God would punish him.

He had been told by his rabbis that if you kill a living being or in any way cause it to die, then when you die and go to hell, your arms and legs are tied to four different horses and a gun is fired into the air and the horses bolt, tearing you to pieces.

He wondered if the rabbis were right.

He wondered if Heimish was watching him from heaven.

"You're disgusting," said Heimish, peering down from the sky. "If it weren't so sinful, it'd be pathetic."

Shlomo switched off the light. He closed his eyes and thought of Candy Cantaloupes. And Mrs. Malinowitz. And the blond porn star car driver

He topped off his afterlife pot of boiling semen and fell asleep.

Holocaust Tips
for Kids

[Parents: Next Tuesday we will be commemorating Holocaust Remembrance Day with an all-day program of films and lectures for students in grades 4-8, much of which will be graphic and potentially disturbing. Please sign and return this permission slip so that your child may attend. Thank you.]

IF the Nazis come in the middle of the night and try to take me away to a concentration camp, these are the things I plan to take with me: some food, my allowance money, a sleeping bag, my Walkman, a toothbrush, a knife from the kitchen, my nunchucks, some Ninja throwing stars, a flashlight and my comic books.

Holocaust means "burned up."

Kristallnacht means "The Night of Broken Glass."

On November 10, 1938, the Nazis broke the Jews' store windows and burned down the shuls. That's why it's called "The Night of Broken Glass."

If ever there's a Night of Broken Glass where you live, leave.

In the movie *Holocaust,* the Weisses waited too long after Kristallnacht to leave. Then they all died, except for their son Rudy. Their other son Karl was sent to Buchenwald.

Buchenwald was one of the largest concentration camps in Germany. It was opened in 1937.

"If you are at lunch, or if you have no appetite to hear

what the Germans have done, now is a good time to switch off the radio, for I propose to tell you of Buchenwald."
—*CBS news, seven years later, in 1945*

The character of Karl Weiss was played by James Woods, who also played one of the Israeli Air Force pilots in the movie *Raid on Entebbe.* In that movie his name was Captain Sammy Berg.

John Saxon was also a pilot in *Raid on Entebbe.* He has a Black Belt in karate. He was in *Enter the Dragon.*

I'll leave right after the next Kristallnacht, and I'll take Deena with me. Her parents won't want her to leave, but if we want to live, we'll have to go right away. There will be no time to waste. We can walk to the highway and hitchhike from there. It's not that far. Maybe Kevin's mom will give us a ride.

We'll probably go to Florida and stay in the Fontainebleau Hotel in Miami. Deena goes there every January with her family. They have a tennis court and a pool.

Florida is 1,330 miles from New York. You need to get to a highway called I-95 South. From there it's a straight drive all the way to Miami.

Kevin isn't Jewish. In the summer, we ride bicycles together. My mother says his mother is a no-good anti-Semite.

In 1934, The New York Times *described the news that Nazis planned to massacre the Jews as "wild rumors."*

Nazis always come in through the front door. They knock loudly. "Shnell!" they shout. That means "quick" in German. Then one of them will kick the door in with his boot. Nazis always wear shiny boots.

GERMAN	ENGLISH
Achtung	Attention
Führer	Leader
Deutschland	Germany
Juden	Jew
Verboten	Forbidden
Hure	Whore

Schweinhund	Swine
Frauen	Women
Kinder	Children

When Rabbi Akiva was being tortured to death by the Romans, his students saw him saying the Shema with joy, oblivious to the pain he was enduring. "How can you be saying Shema with joy," asked his students, "oblivious to the pain you are enduring?" Rabbi Akiva said he was happy to be able to obey God with all his life.

There are three ways out of my house other than the front door, depending on where you are when the Nazis break in:

1. The back door, which leads to the backyard.
2. The door in the living room, which leads onto the deck.
3. The fire escape ladder beside my bedroom window.
   (Note: My bedroom window faces the front of the house, so make sure all the Nazis have already gone into the house before going down the ladder or they'll see you.)

The best hiding places in my house are: at the top of the tall linen closet at the end of the hallway, inside the clothing hamper in the laundry room (try to cover yourself with the clothes), upstairs in the attic behind the summer boxes and under the green couch in the den (if you can fit).

Anne Frank hid in her attic for over two years.

Maybe I should pack more food.

You can also hide in the tree house in my backyard. I doubt the Nazis will check every tree house in America.

It will probably be difficult for them to climb trees in those boots.

Ninjas could make themselves invisible.

"Absorb whatever is useful." —Bruce Lee

Maybe Kevin will let me and Deena hide in his attic.

Anna Weiss was the daughter in the movie *Holocaust*. She was sixteen, and she and her mother hid from the Nazis in a room in Inga's house. Inga was married to Karl (Anna's brother) who got sent to Buchenwald. Anyway, one night, Anna got angry at her mother for not leaving Germany when she had the chance. She yelled at her mother and ran outside. Then the Nazis raped her.

In *Enter the Dragon*, Bruce Lee's sister is about to be raped by some gangsters so she kills herself. Bruce Lee finds out that a guy named Han was behind the attack on his sister, so he kills Han and beats up Han's army.

Anna Weiss had a point.

POLL TAKEN IN THE UNITED STATES, JUNE 1944:

Consider the Germans a threat:	*6 percent*
Consider the Japanese a threat:	*9 percent*
Consider the Jews a threat:	*24 percent*

These are some of the things in your house you could use as weapons: pens, pencils, scissors, a handsaw, screwdrivers, a baseball bat, a rolling pin from the kitchen, salt for throwing in Nazis' eyes, knives, forks, a hammer, toothpicks for stabbing, a blowtorch, lightbulbs for throwing, the hard end of a toothbrush, a pointy-handled comb, an ice pick, the ax, a sledgehammer, the lighter fluid from behind the barbecue that you could spray on them and then throw a match at, a shovel, the pick, a trowel, the cultivator rake, nails, screws, razor blades, sewing needles, safety pins, chisels and knitting needles.

Jews were expelled from England in 1290, France in 1306, Hungary in 1349, France again in 1394, Austria in 1421, Lithuania in 1445, Spain in 1492, Portugal in 1497 and Moravia in 1744.

Some ballpoint pens have replaceable ink cartridges. If you take the cartridge out and put a sewing needle in, you can shoot it out like a Ninja blowgun.

Rabbi Brier says that the Holocaust happened because the Jews assimilated.

That's also why Hashem made the Jews slaves in Egypt.

And why He let the Holy Temple be destroyed by the Romans.

King Solomon built the first Holy Temple. Then the Babylonians destroyed it and deported all the Jews. Seventy years later, a second temple was built. Then the Romans destroyed it and deported all the Jews.

There was no third temple.

Assimilating is when you stop being Jewish, like Woody Allen.

My mother says Woody Allen is a self-hating Jew.

The Talmud teaches that every tear that is shed by a Jew contributes in heaven to the building of the next temple.

The temple in China where they taught karate was called the Shaolin Temple. In *The Chinese Connection*, Bruce Lee plays a student who goes back to his school and finds his teacher dead. He finds out the Japanese did it and he goes to their school; he beats them all up and kills anyone who had anything to do with the killing. The best parts are when he fights a big Russian guy and also when he smashes a Japanese sign that says NO DOGS OR CHINESE ALLOWED.

My favorite Bruce Lee movie is *Game of Death*, where Bruce Lee fights Kareem Abdul-Jabbar.

Kareem Abdul-Jabbar is a Muslim.

Muslims say that Jews are the sons of dogs and pigs.

Between 1938 and 1944, over 1.5 million children under the age of sixteen were murdered by the Nazis.

HOW TO BUILD NUNCHUCKS:

1. Take an old broomstick and cut off two sixteen-inch pieces.
2. Drill a hole through each one roughly one inch down from the end.

3. Put a string through the two holes and tie the
   ends together.

James Caan is Jewish. He was Sonny in the movie
The Godfather.

Art Garfunkel from Simon and Garfunkel looks a
lot like Sonny, and he's also Jewish.

Mercedes and BMW used Jewish prisoners from
Buchenwald to build their cars.

So did Ford.

Bayer gave chemicals to Josef Mengele to use for
the experiments he was doing to the Jews. He would
cut your leg open and put dirt and pieces of glass
into the cut just to see what happened to you.

Jews shouldn't buy Mercedes or BMWs. Or Fords.

Sometimes, though, we buy Bayer aspirin.

Deena's parents have two Mercedes and a pool.

Last year, her sister and mother both had nose jobs.

Deena also wants a nose job but her mother says not until she's sixteen.

My mother says nose jobs are for people who are ashamed to be Jewish.

If you put double-sided tape around the top of your penis and pull the skin up around it, you can tell the Nazis that you're not a Jew.

During the Inquisition, thousands of Jews were murdered simply for refusing to convert to Christianity.

"And now," says Rabbi Brier, "you're going to violate the Shabbos?"

Houdini was also Jewish. His real name was Erich Weiss. He was an escape artist. One time they locked him in a box and put him underwater and he still managed to escape. The box was even locked from the outside.

They called him the King of Handcuffs.

To make yourself look like a Nazi, you can dye your hair blond. Your hair will still be black underneath, so you're not really assimilating.

After Kristallnacht, 30,000 Jews were put on cattle cars and sent to concentration camps. Many people suffocated before they even got there.

When they put you in a cattle car, try to get a spot near a window.

Cattle cars are locked from the outside.

Houdini's father was a rabbi. He had his own synagogue in Wisconsin.

When the cattle car comes to a stop, the Nazis will make you get out. If you are sick, they will send you to the death camps; if you are healthy, they will send you to the work camps.

You need to be in good shape for the Holocaust.

Houdini ran ten miles every day.

Bruce Lee ran six miles every day. For meals he mixed milk, eggs, meat and the blood of cows in a blender.

If you're kosher you can't have meat in your milk-shake.

A famous rabbi was taken from his home by the Nazis and sent to a slave labor camp. The Nazis decided to make an example of him. In front of all the Jews, they took him outside and ordered him to eat a piece of nonkosher meat or they would kill him. "I will not eat this meat," the rabbi said. The Nazis shot him in the head.

"And you," says Rabbi Brier, "you want to eat a cheeseburger."

Fifty thousand Jews were murdered in Austria. Three hundred thousand Jews were murdered in Romania. One hundred and forty thousand Jews were murdered in Germany. Three million Jews were murdered in Poland.

Kevin's family is originally from Poland.

HOW TO MAKE A BOMB FROM A TENNIS BALL:

1. Drill a hole in the tennis ball.
2. Fill the tennis ball with lots of broken-off match heads.
3. When you throw the ball, the match heads rub together and ignite, and the ball explodes.

Sandy Koufax was a Jew. He was a pitcher for the Dodgers.

Q: How do you know if the firing squad is Polish?
A: They're standing in a circle.

One way to survive a firing squad is to fall into the ditch just a split second before the Nazis start shooting. Then, just wait until dark and climb out.

A lot of the people in the Holocaust movies moan and groan in the pit; if you do that they'll come over and shoot you, so just be quiet and act dead.

Bruce Lee could kill a man three different ways with just one blow:
1. A karate punch to the temple.

2. A karate chop to the throat.
3. An uppercut to the nose.

The ancient Egyptians said that all Jews were lepers. Two thousand years later, so did Voltaire. A hundred years later, so did Karl Marx.

Rabbi Brier said that when the Jews were fleeing Egypt, the dogs didn't bark at them and that's why dogs are rewarded with heaven.

The Nazis trained their dogs to bite the Jews.

Hitler's dog was named Blondie.

Voltaire was a founder of something called the Enlightenment.

Nazi dogs don't go to heaven.

You have surpassed all nations in impertinent fables, in bad conduct, and in barbarism. You deserve to be punished, for this is your destiny. —Voltaire

Karl Marx's father was Jewish.

Groucho Marx was Jewish. His real name was Julius Henry Marx. Chico's name was Leonard.

The Nazis did not discern between observant and nonobservant Jews. Anyone with three Jewish grandparents was considered a Jew.

"And you," says Rabbi Brier, "you think you can just take off your yarmulke."

Kevin calls my yarmulke a beanie. I am a Beanie Boy.

If Kevin becomes a Nazi, the first place he'll tell the SS to look for me and Deena is in his attic. But we'll be in Florida.

Anne Frank was murdered in Bergen-Belsen after someone reported the family to the Nazis, so really—don't tell anyone where you are going.

They're not really showers.

They'll probably make New York City into a ghetto, like the Warsaw Ghetto. If you live in a big city where there are Jews and one day there's a Holocaust, you should leave right away.

These are the other cities I think they'll make into ghettos: Los Angeles, Philadelphia, Chicago, Boston and San Francisco.

London, too, if they take over England.

America in German is 'Amerika.'

The rabbis showed us a movie called *Ambulance*. Some Jewish kids and their schoolteacher are forced into the back of an ambulance. The doctors lock them in, attach a hose from the exhaust pipe of the truck to the back door of the ambulance and drive away.

The world record for holding your breath is eight minutes and six seconds. Some people said Houdini could hold his breath for twelve minutes.

If you take a glass bottle, fill it with gasoline, shove a rag into the bottle and light it, you can throw it and it explodes like a bomb.

Before the Romans burned Rabbi Chananya at the stake, they wrapped his body in a Torah scroll and placed tufts of water-soaked cotton around his heart to delay his death and prolong his suffering.

Houdini's cousin was married to Moe from *The Three Stooges.* Moe's real name was Moses Horowitz. He was Jewish.

So were Larry and Curly.

The Mishnah says that it was our forefather Isaac who asked God to bring suffering to the world, since suffering is a great thing. God replied that it is indeed a wonderful idea and so He made Isaac blind.

Who would want to kill the Stooges?

Sometimes the Nazis set their dogs loose on the Jews who weren't dead yet.

To stop a dog from attacking you, shove a finger up its butt.

Ninjas called that the Hidden Leaf Technique.

I heard that Billy Idol is a Nazi.

David Bowie, too.

Houdini's father was fired from his congregation for being too religious.

Cuba turned away a boat full of 1,000 Jewish refugees. So did the United States. And Turkey. Switzerland sent back 30,000.

In 1492 the Jews were expelled from Spain. The Moors turned them away, too.

At the end of the war, Hitler killed himself.

When the Americans liberated Dachau, the bodies in the ovens were still burning.

A lot of the American soldiers who freed the camps were black.

If you are black and Nazis take over, they'll make you get sterilized. That means you can't have children.

Before Hitler killed himself, he killed his dog Blondie because he didn't want her to suffer.

In a 1943 Gallup poll, 30 percent of people dismissed the news that 2 million Jews had been killed in Europe as a rumor.

Karl Brandt was a Nazi doctor. They hung him for war crimes. "It is no shame to stand on this scaffold," he said.

During the Holocaust, a Nazi doctor named Klaus Schilling infected a thousand Jews with malaria. "Please," he said at the Nuremberg trials, "let me finish my experiments."

A German officer once went to the Passover Seder of a local rabbi. The Seder service was very long, and the German officer was getting very hungry. Finally, the rabbi's wife brought out a tray full of food. The German took one bite and spat it out. "What a stupid people!" he shouted. "Waiting all this time, just to eat bitter herbs!" The German officer walked angrily out the door. "What a fool," said the rabbi. "If only he had waited a moment more, the bitter herbs would have been followed by a delicious meal."

"And that," says Rabbi Brier, "is the whole history of the Jews."

Our families will come to Miami, too, if they haven't all been murdered in the camps. Then we'll buy a big house with a tennis court and a pool and a car that's not a Mercedes or a Ford, and maybe if Kevin isn't a Nazi he can come visit us and we can ride bikes on the beach or something.

Seven years after the Holocaust, 400,000 Russian Jews were sent to labor camps in Siberia.

Today, *Mein Kampf* is a bestseller in the Middle East.

Graffiti in Germany:	*"Six million was not enough."*
Graffiti in France:	*"Death to the Jews."*
Graffiti in America:	*"Israel = Nazis."*

Most of the time, Houdini had the keys.

Most of *Game of Death* where Bruce Lee fights Kareem Abdul-Jabbar wasn't really Bruce Lee. He was already dead.

TIPS FOR HITCHHIKING:

1. Make a big sign.
2. Stand at the entrance to a highway.
3. Smile.
4. Stand where there's space for a car to pull over.
5. If you can, bring a girl along, like Deena.

Florida is 6,600 miles from Israel. We'll probably go to Jerusalem and stay in the King David Hotel. Deena goes there every Passover with her family. They have a tennis court and a pool.

Waiting for Joe

IN the beginning, he was always on time. But it had been a long time since the beginning, longer than either Doughnut or Danish could remember.

"I don't get it," complained Danish. "Isn't it time?"

"It's time," answered Doughnut.

"It feels like it's time."

"It's time."

Danish paced anxiously back and forth. Of course it was time! He knew it was time! He didn't need Doughnut to tell him that it was time!

"So where is he then?" asked Danish. "If it's time, then where is he? I don't understand. Either he knows that it's time or he doesn't. Does he know that it's time?"

Doughnut sat curled up inside their cold, empty feeding bowl, focused intently on the doorknob of the apartment front door, believing with all of his heart that at any moment the doorknob would turn, the door would open and Joe would appear.

"We cannot pretend to think that we know what Joe knows and what Joe doesn't know," pronounced Doughnut with a sharp twitch of his nose, "we must only believe with all of our heart that Joe knows."

"I bet he doesn't know!" said Danish. He rose up on his hind legs and flailed uselessly at the glass walls until he became exhausted. Breathing heavily, he lumbered over to the water bottle that hung in the far corner and drew a few drops into his mouth.

"You nonbelievers are all the same," scoffed Doughnut. He pushed some dry cedar chips into a small, comfortable mound and settled down upon it. "As if you were the first hamster to ever doubt him!" he said. "The first rodent to ever *think*, really. Who else but you—with your keen intellect, your contrarian insight, your moral bravery and conviction—who else could possibly come up with,

'What if Joe doesn't?' 'What if Joe can't?' Clothe your fear as integrity, Danish, but Joe knows who believes and Joe knows who doesn't. Joe is here, Joe is there, Joe is simply everywhere. 'What if he never comes back! What if he's forgotten us! What if he's died!' You look around at all your plastic tube high-ways, and your fabulous Habitrail and think you are special. But do ants not build anthills? Do bees not build hives? It is not what we build that makes us unique, it is what we believe; it is that we believe at all! Doubt, my dear Danish, is no great achieve-ment; it is faith that sets us apart. Besides," added Doughnut, "he left his wallet on the front table. He's got to come back."

"He did?" asked Danish.

He stood up on his back legs and squinted through the glass. "Where?"

Doughnut walked over and stood beside Danish.

"There, on the table."

"Where?"

"There!"

"That?"

"Yes!"

"That's not a wallet, you idiot."

"Of course it's a wallet."

"It's a book," said Danish.

"It's not a book."

"Sure it is," said Danish. "I can read the spine. *Along Came a Spider*, by James Patterson." He dropped down and shook his head. "Oh, no, he does not."

Doughnut squinted a moment longer.

Damn.

It was a paperback.

Why would Joe abandon them? Why would he leave a sign for them right there on the foyer table, and then make it not a sign? And why James Patterson? What did it all mean?

"He does not read James Fucking Patterson!" cried Danish. "Our Salvation! Our Provider! We must be out of our minds."

"It's a test," Doughnut said, as he curled back up in bed. "He's testing our faith."

Danish stood on his hind legs and flailed uselessly at the glass wall until he became exhausted. He took a drink of water, climbed up into the plastic tree house and curled into a tight, angry ball.

"I happen to find Patterson thought-provoking and suspenseful," Doughnut said after a moment.

"You what?" asked Danish. "Did you just say you find James Patterson thought-provoking and suspensful? Jesus Christ. Open your eyes, Doughnut. Don't you see what he's doing to us? Holding our food over our heads like this? Dangling our fate before us like a banana-raisin-nut bar tied to the end of a stick? Look at you, Doughnut. Are you so desperate to believe in Joe that you're actually defending James Patterson?!!"

"*Cat and Mouse* was a taut psychological thriller," said Doughnut.

"Oh, bullshit," said Danish.

Doughnut closed his eyes. Hunger stabbed sharply at his stomach, but he would never admit it to Danish.

Where the hell was Joe?

Danish rummaged frantically through the seed shells and shavings that covered the floor of their transparent little world. "He isn't coming!" he said, looking for even a sliver of a husk of a shell of a seed. "He isn't coming."

Doughnut nestled deeper into his bed, eyes shut tight in fervent concentration.

"May he who has fed us yesterday," he prayed, "feed us again today and tomorrow and forever. Amen."

"Yes!" Danish suddenly shouted. "Ya ha!" He pulled a brown chunk of apple from beneath a small mound at the back of the cage and raised it victoriously overhead. Without even stopping to knock off the stray bits of cedar and pine needle that stuck to its sides, Danish opened his mouth wide and dropped it in. He made quite a show of chewing it, mmming and ohhing and ahhhing, finally swallowing it with a loud, dramatic gulp. He smiled, patted his stomach and burped, a deep, long belch of satisfaction. "Aah." He washed it down with a few drops of water and slid down to the floor with a contented sigh.

Doughnut watched Danish, a sour mix of jealousy and disdain on his face. His stomach groaned.

Where the hell was Joe?

Doughnut stood up and stomped over to Danish, who looked up at him lazily.

"Well?" demanded Doughnut.

"Well what?"

"Well, maybe you could give a little thanks," said Doughnut.

"Thanks?" asked Danish. "To who?"

"To Joe, Danish. To Joe."

"For what?"

"For the apple he gave you."

"The apple *he* gave *me*?" asked Danish. "I found that apple myself."

"Do you think the apple just grew there?" Doughnut shouted. "How did the apple get there, Danish? We searched this cage a thousand times and never found a thing. That apple was a miracle! A gift! Joe heard my prayers, and he brought forth upon this cage a holy apple."

His stomach grumbled.

Danish belched again, and rubbed his belly with pride. "Except, Doughnut, that you didn't get any food. You asked, I received. Seems like a strange system to me." He sucked a piece of apple rind out from between his teeth. "Mmm, not that I'm complaining. Next time ask him for a carrot. I simply *must* start getting more fiber."

"Joe grants food to those who need it most," replied Doughnut bitterly.

Danish tired quickly of Doughnut's lectures, particularly when he was hungry, which he suddenly was.

Again.

He got back up and began searching again through the rough cedar chips that covered the floor.

Doughnut dragged himself wearily back to his bed. The miracle of the apple had made him ravenous.

Doughnut would never admit it—he was ashamed to even think it—but lately he'd begun to doubt.

Lately, Joe and his mysterious ways were beginning to piss him off. It was the same thing with him every damn day: begging, thanks, begging. Verse, chorus, verse.

"Why me?" wondered Doughnut.

It must have been his own fault.

He must have sinned.

He must have angered Joe.

Just last week he had questioned why their litter wasn't changed more frequently.

"Perhaps there's a cedar shortage?" he'd asked Danish sarcastically. "It is a hardwood, you know."

He had even complained aloud that their cage was too small.

The chutzpah!

Some hamsters don't even have a cage, let alone a Habitrail and an exercise wheel! How could he have been so ungrateful? He barely even used the blessed exercise wheel. A beautiful exercise wheel that any hamster would love, and Doughnut had only ever used it once.

He was ashamed of himself.

No wonder there wasn't any food!

Why should Joe give him anything more, if he couldn't even appreciate what he had already been given?

Doughnut closed his eyes and silently thanked Joe for starving him in order to show him the error of his ways.

"Forgive me," he prayed.

And with that Doughnut hurried out of his bed and climbed onto the exercise wheel. He ran as fast as he could, huffing and puffing, regret and retribution nipping at his heels.

Danish, meanwhile, was going mad. He'd been tricked. Tricked by Joe! He was even hungrier now than he'd been before he had eaten Joe's cursed apple.

"Oh, yes, very good, Joe, yes, quite witty!" shouted Danish. "Well done, old boy! Touché!"

Back on the exercise wheel, Doughnut could run no more. He stumbled back to bed.

Danish stood on his hind legs and flailed uselessly at the glass walls until he became exhausted.

Doughnut prayed.

And behold, suddenly, the doorknob did turn.

The apartment door did open.

And Joe did appear.

Danish peed in excitement.

Doughnut shat in fear.

Joe was thin and pale, and he wore a rumpled brown suit and a horizontal-striped clip-on tie. The badge hanging from his chest pocket read MAIL-ROOM. There was a woman with him, too, a woman Danish and Doughnut had never seen before. She was unattractive, with thin hair and thick glasses, and she and Joe wrestled their way through the doorway as one, groping and feeling and rubbing each other as if each had somehow lost the keys in the other's pants pockets. Joe groaned and tore open her blouse.

Danish and Doughnut pressed their noses to the glass.

"There better be apples in there," said Danish.

"Forgive me, Joe, for doubting you," prayed Doughnut.

Joe lifted the woman into his arms. "To hell with dinner!" he whispered lustfully. She threw her head back and laughed, and as they headed down the hallway toward his bedroom, Joe switched the living room lights off with his elbow.

Darkness.

Doughnut looked at Danish.

Danish looked at Doughnut.

"We have brought this upon ourselves," said Doughnut.

Danish stood on his hind legs and flailed uselessly at the glass walls until he became exhausted.

Doughnut prayed.

Startling
Revelations
from the
Lost Book of Stan

STANLEY FISHER—down on his luck, out of a job, and with a baby on the way—took the last of his dwindling savings, kissed his wife Sharon goodbye and journeyed to Israel for a soul-searching expedition through the Negev Desert.

He sought meaning.

He sought guidance.

He sought purpose.

What he found was much more important.

Deep inside a dark cave on the dark side of a dark and desolate mountain range, Stanley discovered thirteen ancient stone tablets whose message, once deciphered, could change the entire course of human existence. They didn't, of course, but they did change the course of Stanley's.

THE world was a dark and depressing place in those days. There were people everywhere. Most of those people considered most of the other people something less than people. All the people wanted all the other people the hell out of their country.

Everybody believed in Someone or Something and whatever anybody believed, they believed it completely. Their belief in their belief was unbelievable. They had complete faith in their faith. The only thing they doubted was doubt itself.

There were two things, however, that everyone believed, no matter what they believed: Whatever they believed was unbelievably right, and what everybody else believed was unbelievably wrong.

Piety and passion were in great supply. Homelands were not.

Arms dealers had never been busier.

It was a dark and depressing place.

•••

Stanley carried the tablets back to his hotel room, stacked them carefully in the corner, and double-locked his door.

They looked ancient.

They looked important.

They looked holy.

"Fuckin' A," said Stanley. He phoned Sharon.

"A million," he guessed. "Maybe a million and a half."

"Mmm hmm," said Sharon.

Stanley had been fired from his job well over a year ago now. Along with their only source of income, they'd also lost their medical insurance.

If only they'd known Sharon was pregnant, they would have continued their old insurance. Now that they knew she was pregnant, they couldn't get new insurance.

She wished they'd known.

He was glad they hadn't.

What would knowing do? Knowing what he knew was already burden enough. He didn't need to know any more.

What Sharon knew was that vaginal births cost around $6,000, and cesareans cost around twelve; complications, said the doctors, would only complicate things. She also knew that the total cost of disposable diapers to potty-train a baby was around $2,000, and that a good baby monitor would easily run you a couple hundred bucks.

"I'll call you when I find a buyer," said Stanley.

"Mmm hmm," said Sharon.

STANLEY brought the tablets to the head of the department of ancient languages at the Hebrew University.

"Momentous," said the head of the department of ancient languages at the Hebrew University.

The tablets, he declared, were without a doubt one of the most important religious and archeological finds if not in the history of all mankind, then certainly in what we now know as the Modern Era.

"Can I quote you?" asked Stanley.

The head of the department of ancient languages at the Hebrew University kicked Stanley in the shin, and caught him with a hard uppercut to the nose. "I have a career to think about, asshole," he said, and chased Stanley around his desk with a copy of *The Unabridged History of Ancient Civilizations* raised menacingly over his head.

Stanley didn't know what the head of the department of ancient languages at the Hebrew University's problem was, but he knew that without expert verification, the tablets were worthless.

"An absolute treasure," said the curator of the archeology department at the Israel Museum. "While their monetary value is undoubtedly in the millions, their social and historical value is unimaginable."

"Millions!" said Stanley. "Can I quote you?"

The curator of the archeology department at the Israel Museum grabbed Stanley in a headlock, beat him about the head and told him to forget they ever met. "I'm a respected professional," said the curator of the archeology department at the Israel Museum, giving Stanley a wedgie and shoving him out of his office.

Everyone seemed to agree.

The tablets were ancient.

The tablets were important.

But they weren't holy. In fact, they were unholy, and their existence potentially unholified quite a few other tablets around the world.

Stanley's tablets were an ancient copy of the Old Testament. There were plenty of ancient Old Testaments around, to be sure, some older than others, but this wasn't just any ancient Old Testament. This was a Very Old Testament. This was an Extremely Old Testament.

As it turned out, this was the Oldest Testament of Them All.

But what troubled both the head of the department of ancient languages at the Hebrew University and the curator of the archeology department at the Israel Museum wasn't the tablets' very old age, or even their very, very old age. What had the experts so utterly and completely freaked out was that the text of this Oldest Testament of Them All was identical to every Not Quite as Old Testament written after it, down to the very last letter, except for one short paragraph at the very top of the very first tablet, a paragraph that seemed to have been dropped from the later editions, a paragraph that simply read:

The following is a work of fiction. Any resemblance to persons living or dead is entirely coincidental.

Which caused a number of problems.

"I'm having a little trouble finding a buyer," Stanley said to his wife.

"Mmm hmm," she said.

The Graco Lite-Rider Stroller/Car Seat Combo

cost $129.99. The Precious Moments Bassinet cost $79.99. The Venetian-style crib in White Oak finish was $399.99.

STANLEY maxed out the last of his credit cards and bought a one-way ticket to Rome. If anyone had the cash for these tablets, the Church did.

"It's a fraud," said the Pope. "A cynical, monstrous fraud of the very worst kind."

"A fraud?" asked Stanley, taking a closer look at the stone tablet lying on the Pontiff's desk. "Are you sure?"

"It has to be," said the Pope.

"It has to be, or it is?"

"It is," said the Pope menacingly, "because it has to be."

And with that, the Pope grabbed his Papal Staff and poked Stanley painfully in his stomach.

"You get me?" the Pope said.

The world was a dark and depressing place in those days.

You are bidding on eBay item #765-876, "The Book of Stan," an ancient Biblical text which calls into

question the veracity of all Bible-based religions includ-
ing Judaism, Islam and Christianity. New baby forces
sale. Buyer agrees to pay shipping.

The response was overwhelming.

"Fuck you, asshole," wrote JesusLvr1. "May God strike you dead as he did the sinners of Sodom and Gomorrah," wrote DaPreacher316. "People like you sicken me," wrote HornyDevil22, "and BTW, how much do you want for your wife's panties?"

Religious leaders around the world were irate. Mankind was already teetering on the brink of self-destruction; this was no time for the truth.

The Church called for an immediate investigation, and by investigation, they meant arrest and prosecution. Primarily pushers of the Testament New, church leaders had a definite interest in the Original remaining divine. If the Old Testament turned out to be nothing more than ancient Babylonian beach reading, what were they to make of Jesus, who claimed the Old Testament was the word of God Himself (Matthew 15:6, "And by this you invalidated the Word of God.")? Was the Book of Stan implying that Jesus was some kind of a liar, or was it implying he was some kind of a schmuck?

"By allowing the absolute authority of the Bible to be challenged," wrote Jerry Falwell on his ministry's website that week, "we as a society have turned our back on God. And click here," he added, "for big savings on all audio cassettes and DVDs." Everything, the Reverend promised, must go.

The Muslims weren't any happier. Allah of Koran fame and Elohim of Old Testament fame are one and the same, and the followers of the Prophet Mohammed did not take kindly to His being deemed either fictional or coincidental. (It must be said, though, that the Shiites were okay with "coincidental" and the Sunnis were okay with "fictional"; unfortunately, each declared the other heretical and seventy people died in clashes throughout the Middle East.) The Ayatollah Khamenei sat down at his tangerine iMac, printed out one copy of "Fatwa.doc," and hastily filled it in.

"Because Stan denies the existence of the Peaceful Loving God of Everlasting Mercy and Compassion," wrote the Ayatollah, "it is incumbent upon us to kill him."

Abraham Foxman called an emergency meeting of the ADL, who called an emergency meeting of the JDL. They didn't really care what the Book of Stan claimed about the divinity of the Old Testament, much as they didn't really care what Jesus or Mohammed claimed about it. However, if the Book of Stan were true, then the Old Testament was not true, and if the Old Testament was not true, the whole idea of Jews as a chosen tribe was not true. Brass tacks: If there were no real tribe, then there were no real Jews, and if there were no real Jews there could be no real anti-Semitism, and if there was no anti-Semitism, then Abe and his staff were shit out of a job.

The Book of Stan, declared Foxman, was a vile, pernicious anti-Semitic tract that needed to be banned, its perpetrators arrested, its publisher abducted and its distributor really, really yelled at.

The government, as it happened, was already on the case.

Stanley's ad was immediately deleted. eBay pulled the ad off its server, and the company posted an important policy update in its place:

> eBay will no longer allow the sale or auction of books claiming to be the Word of God, or claiming to not be the Word of God, or books that claim that other books claiming to be the Word of God are not.

And then Stanley was deleted. His birth certificate was destroyed, his medical records burned, his Social Security number reassigned, his parents killed, his sisters raped and his coworkers fired.

"Are you Mrs. Stanley Fisher?" the man at the door asked.

"I am," said Sharon.

"No, you're not."

"I'm not?"

"You can't be," said the man.

"I can't be or I'm not?"

"You're not" said the man menacingly, "because you can't be."

"Mmm hmm," said Sharon.

BACK in Rome, with no foreseeable buyers for his ancient tablets, Stanley got on a plane and headed back to the United States, where he was immediately arrested by immigration officials for using a fake passport.

"It wasn't fake three weeks ago," said Stanley.

"It's fake now."

"How could it be fake?"

"How could it be real?" said the officer.

"Because I'm real," said Stanley.

"That's what you say."

Two men in black suits and sunglasses appeared at his side. One man grabbed the suitcases containing the tablets, while the other led Stanley down the hallway into a small, secluded office. The door was closed, the lock was turned, and that was the end of Stanley Fisher and his troublesome nonfakes.

That evening, the head of the department of ancient languages at the Hebrew University appeared on *The O'Reilly Factor*. It was not just a fake, he said, it was the worst fake, if not in all the history of mankind, then certainly in what we now know as the Modern Era.

"Utterly worthless," added the curator of the archeology department at the Israel Museum, "and not just financially, but to mankind as a whole."

The Pope, on a live video feed from the Vatican, agreed. "It's a fraud," the Pontiff said. "A cynical, monstrous fraud of the very worst kind."

O'Reilly thanked them all, and reminded his viewers that the one book they could buy that definitely wasn't a fake was his book, which was currently number one on the *New York Times* bestseller list. It made, he noted, a wonderful gift.

SHARON was rushed to the hospital. Her water had broken, and she was going into labor.

"Insurance?" asked the nurse.

"None," said Sharon.

"Father?" asked the nurse.

"None," said Sharon.

"Mmm hmm," said the nurse.

Drudge was the first to break the story. "Immaculate Conception in Long Island!" shouted his web page.

The response was overwhelming.

"God bless you and the Son of God," wrote Jesus-Lvr1. "May the Eternal bless you as He did the Virgin Mary," wrote DaPreacher 316. "People like you inspire me," wrote HornyDevil22, "and BTW, how much do you want for your panties?"

Religious leaders around the world were ecstatic. Mankind was already on the brink of self-destruction; a heartwarming fraud like this would do everyone good.

Reverend Falwell welcomed the reports of the

virgin birth, and marked all his merchandise down an additional 15 percent.

The Ayatollah praised the news, calling it the Merciful Hand of Allah, which would soon reach out and destroy Israel.

And Abraham Foxman announced that such a miracle once and for all proved the Jews were the chosen people, and anyone who denied it must surely be an anti-Semite.

Sharon was still without health coverage, but her homeowner's policy included full coverage for acts of God, which her pregnancy clearly was.

Prudential paid for all her medical bills, plus a two-bedroom addition to the house, including a lovely nursery for the baby and a cozy, glass-enclosed porch overlooking the yard.

She was given charity by the 700 Club and clothing and food by the Islamic Society of North America. The UJA provided around-the-clock child-care help in the form of a Filipino nanny named Carmalita. Sean Hannity donated a portion of his Hannitized coffee mug sales to her, and President Bush invited her and the miracle baby to his next State of the Union Address, where he planned to announce a Constitutional amendment protecting virgin births.

And then one day, a few months after Sharon's miraculous delivery, the phone rang.

"Who is this?" Sharon asked.

She could hear breathing on the line. It seemed a long time before the man spoke.

"It's Stanley."

"Stanley?"

"Stanley Fisher."

"There is no Stanley Fisher," said Sharon.

"I'm Stanley Fisher."

"You're not Stanley Fisher," said Sharon.

"I'm not?"

"You can't be," said Sharon.

"I can't be or I'm not?"

"You're not," said Sharon, "because you can't be."

And she hung up the phone.

The world was a dark and depressing place in those days. But the baby cooed happily from inside the Graco Lite-Rider Stroller/Car Seat Combo, the deliverymen were carrying in the new Italian leather couches, and the tile man was already hard at work in the new master bath.

One Death to Go

CHAIM YANKEL ROSENBERG lived in the Sheepshead Bay section of Brooklyn, roughly 5,693 miles from the remote hilltop somewhere between Jerusalem and Tel Aviv where a small group of Kabbalists had gathered to figure out the exact timing of the end of the world.

They should not have been doing that.

This was not the Kabbalah of Roseanne or Madonna. This was the mysticism of Maimonides, of the Ari Zall, of Luzzato. This was Infinite God, creation ex nihilo, Divine Providence. This was some heavy shit.

They gathered in a darkened classroom of their

yeshiva, surrounded by piles of tattered books, reams of wrinkled notes and gallons of black coffee. The night before, they had stumbled on a hidden code which revealed that at the beginning of creation, God had picked A Number.

It was a deal He'd cut with Himself, nervous as he was about this new venture called Man.

A failsafe, really.

The Number the Kabbalists had discovered buried in the ancient text was the number of violent deaths that God would allow to occur in the world before He got fed up and just pulled the plug.

That's all, folks.

Thanks for playing.

Coming this fall, version 2.0.

It seemed a wise plan at the time, and the angels, never big fans of the Mankind project to begin with, backed it heartily. Recently, though, a growing minority had begun to suggest that instead of picking a number in the high million billions, He probably should have picked a number closer to, say, twenty-two, or twelve, or seven.

According to the Kabbalists' calculations, as of last night humanity was just one hundred deaths away from The End.

The Kabbalists were worried, and to make matters worse, they were completely out of cigarettes. Humanity's only shot—and it was a long one—was peace. No wars, no murders, no exceptions. No gang shootings, no assaults with a deadly weapon, no strangulations.

One hundred chances.

The next morning, they issued a press release to every country, every news agency and every law enforcement organization on the planet.

They sent it to Ariel Sharon, and they sent it to Yassir Arafat. They sent it to the leaders of Hamas and to the leaders of Hezbollah and to the leaders of Al Qaeda. They sent it to Rummy, they sent it to Colin and they sent it to Condi. They sent it to Bush Forty-One, who sent it to Bush Forty-Four. They sent it to the Bloods, who sent it to the Crips. They sent it to the Yakuza who kindly forwarded it to the Italian mafia who kindly forwarded it to the Russian mafia who kindly forwarded it to the Israeli mafia.

Sunday morning, the Kabbalists appeared on *Meet the Press* with Tim Russert. "Will you say on this program," said Tim, "with the eyes of the nation upon you, that if one hundred more people die of unnatural causes, the world will cease to exist?"

"Yes," said the Kabbalists.

"One hundred?" reiterated Tim.

"One hundred," said the Kabbalists.

"The whole world?" reiterated Tim.

"The whole world," said the Kabbalists.

The following night on Letterman, the Number One Thing the Kabbalists Don't Know was "Where Did I Leave That Damn Remote?" Leno opened with the Dancing Kabbalists, which everyone felt vaguely uncomfortable about, and the next morning Abraham Foxman filed a formal complaint.

The Kabbalists returned home to pray.

The first ten deaths came that very first night: six rapes and four robberies, all ending in homicide. The next five were shootings, which the D.A. swore he would prosecute as hate crimes, which wouldn't make a difference to the final count either way.

The ten after that were all killed by a Palestinian suicide bomber in Haifa. The United States condemned the bombing, the U.N. censured it and Arafat denounced it. It wouldn't make a difference to the final count either way.

Deaths Twenty-Five to Forty were assorted drive-bys, muggings and stabbings "by a person or persons known to the victim," while deaths Forty to Fifty-Five were unavoidable civilian casualties during a military peacekeeping mission somewhere in Africa. The next twenty were the result of a night of New York City wildings, and another ten rapes and fourteen armed liquor store robberies later, humanity was one death away from The End.

That one was named Chaim Yankel Rosenberg.

The same Chaim Yankel Rosenberg who was, at the moment, 5,693 miles away from the Kabbalists, trembling uncontrollably in a darkened Brooklyn alleyway, reaching into his coat pocket to pull out his wallet for the man holding the steel forty-five-caliber handgun to the back of his head.

Chaim Yankel began to sob.

"Please, in the name of Hashem, don't . . ."

Chaim Yankel didn't know anything about the Kabbalists. He didn't know anything about the End of Days. He knew he was a father of three small children, and he knew he was married to a frail and frightened woman who would not be able to bear his death, let alone raise their family in his sudden absence. He knew that he wanted to see Yitzi's bar mitzvah and he knew that he wasn't going to, because Chaim Yankel also knew that this meshuginah shvartza was going to shoot him in the head no matter what he said or did.

The meshuginah shvartza, for his part, didn't know anything about the Kabbalists either. He knew that if he didn't get the money for Latrell, he was going to get shot in the head himself. He knew that his baby girl wasn't going to have a daddy unless Daddy came up with the cash for Latrell. He knew that the odds of a black man in America living past the age of forty were something like a hundred to one. He knew for damn sure that if he let this fucking kike live, he'd go right to the fucking police with his fucking lawyer, which in his experience was just another word for a fucking kike.

There was a loud popping sound, and the last thought to cross Chaim Yankel Rosenberg's mind was, "Son of a bitch, he shot me."

He was hoping to say Shema.

Chaim Yankel was only partially correct. The meshuginah shvartza did shoot him in the head, but later that same night he also killed a convenience store clerk in Queens, shot a liquor store owner in the Bronx and carjacked a couple of accountants in a silver Cadillac Escalade.

All told, according to the police blotters in the next day's *Post*, there were seventeen murders that night. "About normal for a Saturday night," an officer was quoted as saying.

Three days later, the Kabbalists issued a formal apology for their regrettable mathematical error. In their haste and excitement, they had inadvertently missed a couple of decimal points. They were contrite and sincere. They begged forgiveness and announced that the new number of violent deaths left before the End of Days was exactly one thousand.

"Minus the nine murders, three drunk drivers, the serial killing in Virginia and four Islamic militants killed last night in a retaliatory strike for the previous night's bombing in Haifa," their press release concluded, "that makes 983 to go."

Later that afternoon, on a shady hill in the B'nei Zion Cemetery overlooking the Brooklyn–Queens Expressway, the Rosenbergs and a few close friends buried their beloved Chaim Yankel.

It was a quiet, respectful service. On their way out, as they passed through the cemetery gates, the

Rosenbergs stopped, and took one last look at Chaim Yankel's grave.

The children waved sadly.

Mrs. Rosenberg blew her husband a kiss.

"We shall be together soon, my love," she whispered to her husband. "I give 'em till Monday, tops."

The Metamorphosis

As Motty awoke one morning from impure dreams he found himself transformed in his bed into a very large goy. In his waking half-sleep, he lazily scratched his hairy chest.

Hairy?

He threw back the covers. His chest had become broad and muscular. A thick coat of curly black hair spread across it and trailed down his stomach. His newly muscular arms and shoulders felt huge in his tank top. Motty didn't remember owning a tank top, certainly not one that said Budweiser across the chest.

Awesome.

He moved his heavy arms up and down, watching the muscles expanding and contracting beneath his suddenly taut skin. Beginning on his shoulder and extending down his arm was an elaborate tattoo of a blond woman in a bikini straddling a large sword that rested in the eye socket of a bloody skull.

He was overcome with the desire to build something with hammers and wood.

He ran to his mirror. From the neck up, nothing had changed. He was all Motty. From the neck down, he was a burly construction worker. It gave the effect of some sort of experimental head reassignment surgery gone terribly wrong. In addition to the tank top, he was wearing a red and black flannel plaid shirt buttoned only to the chest, and faded denim jeans, torn at the knees, from which hung a yellow and black Stanley tape measure marked "Contractor Grade." Motty unzipped the jeans and looked inside his black underwear. Black underwear?

"So that's a foreskin."

It occurred to Motty that somewhere out there was a once-burly, previously uncircumcised construction-type person running around with the body of an eighteen-year-old Lubavitcher yeshiva student.

"But," thought Motty, "that's his problem." He stopped himself. "That's his *fuckin'* problem."

Nice.

There was a loud rapping on his bedroom door. "You're going to be late for shul!" his mother shouted. "Motty!" He had completely forgotten it was Shabbos.

Motty swung the door open.

"Ta-da!"

Motty's massive goyish body filled the doorway. His mother's mouth dropped open in a silent scream. Her eyes rolled backward into her head, her eyelids fluttered and she fell face first onto the hard bedroom floor.

She was out cold.

Motty lifted her up and carried her to her bedroom. He put her in bed, installed some ceramic tile in the master bath and left for shul.

With his goyishe legs and powerful stride, it took him only half the usual time to reach the synagogue, but he still walked in right in the middle of the rabbi's midservice sermon.

Everyone turned.

"Who dares to walk in right in the middle of the rabbi's speech?" their faces all seemed to ask.

A tall shaygitz in jeans wearing a yarmulke and a tallis was not the answer they were expecting.

The chief rabbi motioned to the cantor, who motioned to the assistant rabbi, who hurried down the aisle to the man in the jeans and motioned to him to please come outside.

"Are you a guest or friend of a current shul member?" asked the assistant rabbi.

Motty explained it all as simply and directly as he possibly could. He was Motty Aranson. He had awakened as a goy, it was as simple as that, but clearly it was a matter of biology and not of belief, and he didn't think it should change anyone's opinion of him.

Motty asked that he please be allowed inside so as not to miss any more of the services.

The assistant rabbi kindly asked that Motty leave the premises before he was forced to call the police.

The doors opened and Rabbi Epstein and Rabbi Akiva stepped outside.

A discussion ensued.

The central question, it seemed, was whether Motty was to be considered kosher or traif. Motty explained that he should be allowed to enter the shul because religion is based on belief, which is a function of thought, which is a function of your brain, which is located in your head. So, Motty observed, the head was more important than the body.

The assistant rabbi disagreed. "When God prohibits the bringing of the flesh of an unfit animal into the Temple, he specifically says flesh. Why? Because God is telling us that no matter how pure the thoughts of the pig might be, his body is still what matters most. We learn from this that the body matters more than the head." Motty's body was prohibited from entering the shul, the assistant rabbi declared; however, if they were to cut Motty's head off, they would certainly be permitted to carry it inside.

Rabbi Epstein shook his head. "Even if we knew for certain," he said, "that a pig had only pure thoughts, and that the pig believed with his whole pig heart in The Holy One Blessed Be His Name, the ancient rabbis still forbid us to eat it." Thus, Rabbi Epstein held, irrespective of whether they could allow Motty into the synagogue, they were, without question, prohibited from eating him.

"That's utterly ridiculous," argued Rabbi Akiva. "If the pig believed in Hashem—as it is written, *With all of your heart and all of your mind*—the ancient rabbis would certainly deem the pig kosher." Therefore, according to Rabbi Akiva, they could not bring Motty into the synagogue, but they could probably eat him. And so it was decided.

"Motty?" the assistant rabbi called out.

But Motty had already gone home.

His mother had still not awakened. He regretted having frightened her so, and decided to prepare the Shabbos lunch for the family so she could rest a bit longer. He also built a second level to the deck and installed some landscape lighting. For entertaining.

He was in the kitchen preparing a kugel tray when he heard his father come through the front door, speaking loudly with a number of other familiar voices.

"I'm in the kitchen!" Motty called out. He recognized the other voices as belonging to Rabbi Brier and Rabbi Falkenstein.

"We didn't see you outside shul," his father was saying, "so we just . . ."

The three men stepped into the kitchen and froze at the sight of him.

Motty tried to explain.

"I woke up like this."

"Shaygitz!" Motty's father spat.

"I'm not a shaygitz!" said Motty, "I'm your son, Motty. Listen! Listen, it's just some kind of a miracle, a Shabbos miracle. I don't know how or why it happened, but I can't see why it should make you feel any diff—"

Motty's father smashed him across the face with his Talmud Bavli. The oversized hardcover book caught Motty just below his left eye, and he fell to the floor.

"Traif!" yelled his father. "You dare to touch our food with your goyishe hands! You anti-Semitic . . ."

He raised the Talmud up to strike the hideous creature again, but Rabbi Brier and Rabbi Falkenstein intervened.

A discussion ensued.

"Rabbi," asked Motty's father, "should not a father correct his son? Is it not written 'Teach them to your children and their children after them?' "

Rabbi Brier explained that while the Torah certainly encourages the hitting of a no-good, rotten child, if the child is traif, you are forbidden from hitting him with a holy book. He suggested that they strike Motty again, only this time with a leather belt, or perhaps a flat piece of unholy wood.

Rabbi Falkenstein disagreed. "Are we not commanded to 'make for yourself a gate out of the Torah?' Could that not be interpreted as permission to use the Torah for your own defense? And is it not true that the best defense is a good offense?"

Rabbi Brier concurred, but added that, if possible, the blows should be concentrated on the head and face, which they knew for certain to be kosher.

Rabbi Falkenstein praised Motty's father for never once hitting his son below the neck, and they all agreed that Motty's father was obligated to continue pummeling Motty with his sacred book. They shook hands, and Rabbi Brier handed Motty's father the Talmud.

"Motty?" his father called out.

But Motty had already gone.

He was on his way to his yeshiva, hoping that at least his friends would accept him. He already knew from the incident at shul that he probably wouldn't be allowed inside the building, so he stood outside and shouted up at the dormitory window.

"Yitzi! Yoel! Yankel!"

They all came outside to meet him.

Motty offered Yankel a handshake, but Yankel held his hands up.

"Traif," Yankel explained.

"Come on, guys, check it out," said Motty, pulling up his sleeve to show them his tattoo. When he flexed his biceps, the woman on the sword seemed to dance. He'd been thinking about getting more ink done.

"Maybe on my back, you know? Eagle wings or something."

Yitzi stepped forward. "Motty, it's a big question if we can still be your friends."

A discussion ensued.

Yitzi explained that he was basing his reasoning on the prohibition from Deuteronomy, "Do not intermarry with them, for they will turn you onto their gods." "If marrying was not allowed," Yitzi put forth, "can we not also assume ipso facto that friendship, too, is prohibited?"

Yoel disagreed. He pointed out that the greater commandment to love your neighbor as you love yourself specifically avoids saying whether the neighbor is Jewish or non-Jewish. Why? "To show us that when it comes to human acts of kindness—such as friendship—religious orientation is of no consequence." According to Yoel, their friendship wasn't merely allowed, it was obligatory.

Yankel argued. "On the contrary," he said. "When Hashem commands us to go to Canaan, He says 'And you shall drive them out of your midst and destroy their idols and images.' What do we learn from this? That not only are we forbidden to be friends with Motty, it is incumbent upon each one of us to kill him."

"Yes," agreed Yitzi. "With a sword."

"Blessed is Hashem," said Yoel, checking his pockets for a sword. "Motty?" he called out, looking around.

But Motty had already gone back home.

He decided he would just leave. Go somewhere else. Even back when his body was Jewish, he'd often suspected that his mind was not.

He could find a place in the city, transfer into NYU, maybe take a film class.

He could find people who would love him for who he was, not for who he was no longer.

When Motty got home, he was met by several officers from the Rockland County Sheriff's Department. They wanted to question him in connection with the death of his mother.

"May I quickly use the bathroom?" Motty asked.

Officer Landry felt that they should not allow him to use the bathroom, as the Sergeant had specifically commanded them to "apprehend" the suspect.

"Yes," argued Officer McKenna, "but is it not written "To Protect and Serve?"

In the living room, the rabbis were debating whether Motty should be punished as a Jew who kills another Jew or as a non-Jew who kills a Jew. Motty walked past, went upstairs, tied a rope tightly around the part of his body where the Jewish part met the goyish part, and quietly hung himself in the shower.

MOTTY sat up in heaven and looked down on his funeral taking place below. A black hearse led the procession, followed closely by his father's beige minivan and a black Lincoln Town Car full of rabbis. They drove all the way to the Gates of Zion Cemetery in Spring Valley, where they were stopped at said gates by the chief of security.

There seemed to be some confusion.

A rabbi from the cemetery office came hurrying down to the gates. His name was Rabbi Pearlstein.

Rabbi Pearlstein was of the opinion that Motty's body could not be buried in a Jewish cemetery because it had a tattoo, though if they were to cut his head off, it would be permissible for them to just bury that.

A discussion ensued.

Motty laughed.

Motty's father looked around. Who was laughing? "Motty?" he called out.

But Motty had already gone.

Prophet's Dilemma

AND behold God spoke to Schwartzman late Tuesday evening, right in the middle of Leno's monologue, saying, "Make for yourself an ark, for you and for your entire family, for I have found you righteous in your generation."

"Now?" asked Schwartzman.

He had to be kidding. It was 11:50 PM on a week night—Schwartzman had an 8:30 with a client the next morning, a 9:30 breakfast with the head of his department and a shrink appointment with Dr. Herschberg at 11:00 which meant that he'd have to catch the 6:00 AM to Grand Central at the latest.

"It's almost *midnight*."

"Shh!" spat Mrs. Schwartzman.

Mrs. Schwartzman liked Jay Leno a lot more than she liked God.

Jay Leno didn't show up at their house at whatever unholy hour he wanted. Jay Leno didn't threaten to wipe humanity from the face of the Earth. Jay Leno didn't tell her husband to build a golden altar in their backyard and sacrifice upon it one she-goat.

Which, by the way, is called a doe.

"Can't we do this in the morning?" whispered Schwartzman.

Mrs. Schwartzman aimed the remote control at the TV set and turned the volume up as high as it would go. She held the button pressed for a few extra seconds—in case He missed the point.

"We'll be right back with more headlines," said Jay.

"I will make you into a great nation," said God, "and I will bless you."

"Yeah, yeah," whispered Schwartzman. "Tomorrow."

•••

IF you ever hear a voice in your head telling you that he's God and he's going to bless you and your children and your children's children, pretend you didn't hear Him.

Schwartzman, like so many others before him, had made the classic mistake.

"Who's that?" he called out when first God spoke to him. "Hello? Who's there? Who's talking?"

Schmuck.

The two long years since had been filled with one ludicrous, Lordly request after another. Slaughter this, banish that. Go there, leave here. Wear this, cut off that. I'll kill you, I'll stone you, I'll flood you.

Then there had been the complaints, of course, mostly from his irate neighbors who would no longer even speak to him.

When he'd applied for a building permit to reconstruct the ancient Babylonian temple in his backyard, the Kleins down the road complained. He'd tried explaining to God the intricacies of residential zoning restrictions, but God wasn't hearing it, and the Kleins eventually filed a restraining order against him.

His letter to the president demanding he "let my people go" brought with it Secret Service surveil-

lance vans on the street and ominous black heli-
copters in the sky; his claim that "God told me to
write that" only brought tabloid reporters and cam-
era crews.

And then there was the morning Mrs. Epstein
opened her bedroom window, looked out the window and saw Schwartzman next door, wrestling a
young goat across the yard and dragging it up the
ramp of a crudely built altar. Cursing and swearing,
Schwartzman finally managed to get the poor animal
to lie down. He lifted a hatchet high above his head
and buried it deep in the she-goat's neck. Blood
sprayed across the lawn. It sprayed onto the swing set,
and onto the deck and onto the white picket fence
separating the Schwartzmans' yard from hers. It took
quite a bit of hacking before the goat's head was finally severed and fell with a thud to the ground.
Covered in blood and drenched in sweat, Schwartzman threw down the hatchet, held out his arms and
looked up to the heavens. "There!" he shouted.
"Happy?"

Mrs. Epstein screamed.

Schwartzman held up his hands. "Just a sin-
offering, Mrs. E!" he called out. "Mrs. E?"

But Mrs. E had already dialed the police.

In the days following, she registered formal complaints with the mayor, the governor and People for the Ethical Treatment of Animals.

A small crowd of animal rights activists met on Schwartzman's lawn. "One, two, three, four! Don't you kill no goats no more!"

This was no way for them to start a family.

THIS is no way for us to start a family," Mrs. Schwartzman had said.

She had made it clear very early on that she didn't want God around when the baby arrived.

"It's difficult enough to raise a child these days," she had said.

She was right. Surly, bossy, paranoid, violent. God was a terrible influence.

"I'll get rid of Him," Schwartzman had promised.

"No, you won't," God had answered.

"Yes, I will," Schwartzman had answered.

And Schwartzman arose early the next morning, and he did call out to God from behind the wheel of his Buick.

"What's an ark, anyway?" Schwartzman asked God as the old engine warmed up.

"It's like a boat," said God.

"What kind of boat? A big boat or a little boat?"

"It's a big boat," said God. "Like a yacht."

Schwartzman owned a hammer, a hatchet, one of those screwdrivers with the x-shaped end and what he strongly suspected was a wrench (it was a vise-grip).

"And I'm supposed to build this yacht? Myself?"

"I built the world by myself," said God.

"Again with the 'I built the world.' "

The guy couldn't go a week without mentioning it.

Lightning flashed, thunder rumbled.

"Behold!" shouted God. "And you shall go forth from this place to the Home Depot on Route 17, or the Lord Your God shall smite you with a consumption, and with a fever, and with an inflammation, and with . . ."

"Yeah, yeah," said Schwartzman, "I know. And with the burning and with the sword and with the blasting."

He put the car in reverse, and slowly backed out of his driveway.

Dick.

...

Excuse me," Schwartzman said to the Home Depot man, "can you tell me where to find tar?"

"Tar?" asked the Home Depot man. "What're you using tar for?"

"I'm building an ark," said Schwartzman.

If there was anything that two years of completing God's preposterous homework assignments had taught Schwartzman it was that there was absolutely nothing you could tell Home Depot Man you were building that would surprise him, that would get any reaction from him at all, for that matter, aside from the usual skepticism about your choice of building materials.

"I wonder if you could help me. I'm building a Babylonian temple. A messianic chariot. An altar for ritual animal sacrifice."

"An altar, eh?" Home Depot Man had asked. "You gonna be using fire on that?"

Home Depot Man shoved the rest of his egg sandwich into his mouth, and wiped his fingers on his orange *"Do-It-Yourself Superstore!"* apron.

"An ark, eh?" he said, licking his fingers.

From Altars to Ziggurats! thought Schwartzman. *From Abraham to Zebediah!*

"What kind of wood you using?" asked Home Depot man.

"Cypress."

"Cypress?"

"That's what the guy wants," said Schwartzman.

"He'd be better off with cedar," said Home Depot Man. "Bug resistant. I'd go with cedar."

WHEN Schwartzman got home, he was met by an angry God and an angrier wife.

"What the hell is this?" demanded God as Schwartzman climbed out of the car.

"It's cedar," he said, slamming the door.

"I know it's cedar," said God, "I wanted cypress."

"What is the big deal?" asked Schwartzman. The guy could be so fucking literal. "It's bug resistant. The guy said to go with cedar."

Ten miles away, at the far end of the Home Depot plumbing and heating aisle, a sixty-gallon water heater rolled off its forty-foot-high shelf and landed squarely on Home Depot Man below, killing him instantly.

"What the hell is this?" demanded Mrs. Schwartzman from the front porch.

"It's cedar," said Schwartzman.

"I know it's cedar," said Mrs. Schwartzman. She turned with a huff and went back into the house, slamming the front door behind her.

Someone's after me," said Schwartzman.

"Mmm hmm," said Dr. Herschberg, scribbling on his note pad.

"He's spoken to me. He won't leave me alone. I've tried to be nice."

"He's spoken to you?"

"He asks me to do Him favors."

"What kind of favors?"

"Favors."

"Have you called the police?"

Dr. Herschberg was a prominent psychiatrist in Manhattan, with a patient list that included many famous New Yorkers. Stalkers were his bread and butter.

Most stalkers, explained Dr. Herschberg, are lonely, isolated members of society, seeking intimacy or friendship. The stalking is simply a partial satisfaction of their voyeuristic, sadistic tendencies.

"That sounds like Him."

"You need to stop responding," said Dr. Herschberg.

"That's what my wife said," replied Schwartzman. "He's not easy to ignore."

"Are you afraid he might become violent?"

"If history's any indication."

Dr. Herschberg leaned forward.

"Every time you respond, you're positively reinforcing his behavior. Every time you answer him, he's getting what he wants."

Schwartzman let out a long, deep breath, and slowly shook his head.

"He's going to be pretty pissed off."

"Exactly," agreed Dr. Herschberg. "And when he gets angry enough, He'll realize you won't give him what he needs, and he'll find a new person to bother."

"And what about that person?"

"They're not my patient."

Schwartzman stared at the floor for a while, thinking hard about what the doctor was suggesting. He looked up at Dr. Herschberg and nodded.

"Okay," he said. "I'll do it. I'll ignore Him."

"No, you won't," said God.

"Yes, I will," said Schwartzman.

"Our time is up," said Dr. Herschberg.

I KNOW you can hear me," God said to Schwartzman through the radio of his car. Six-speaker, Surround Sound divination. Dolby harassment. "It's not going to work."

Schwartzman tried changing the radio station.

Howard Stern was interviewing a lesbian midget. There was a harsh crackle of electrical interference, Howard's voice cut out and behold, God spoke again.

"Hey, Schwartzman," said God. "Listen. I'll tell you a little secret, okay? But you can't tell anyone. It's just between me and you, okay? Because I love you. I do. All right, here goes. It's nature. Nurture's got nothing to do with it! But you can't tell any—"

Schwartzman angrily switched the radio off.

Ten miles away, in the oak-walled office of Dr. Herschberg, a hardcover *Physician's Desk Reference* slid off the highest shelf of the tallest bookcase, striking the doctor on the head and killing him instantly.

SUNDAY morning, Schwartzman was having the golf game of his life.

"I shall bring floodwaters on the earth," shouted God loudly as Schwartzman was trying to line up a putt on the ninth green, "and destroy all that is under heaven! Flinch! Fliiiinch!"

Schwartzman kept his head down, his elbow straight, and sank the putt.

Over the next two weeks, every stock in Schwartzman's portfolio tanked.

He was mugged, carjacked and burglarized. He lost on every scratch-off card he played. He almost won two dollars at Pick Ten, but the winning numeral, 1, mysteriously transformed into a 7.

One morning he found his car with four flat tires. That afternoon, he was rear-ended on the Brooklyn-Queens Expressway. That evening, he dropped his wallet somewhere in Prospect Park while walking his beloved dog Sparky. That night, Sparky was struck by lightning and killed.

"Damnedest thing," said the policeman standing over the sizzling corpse. "And you say his name was Sparky? Damnedest thing."

His cat Millie was run over by a Federal Express truck and the hamsters he kept in the basement escaped from their cages. They quickly took advantage of their long-awaited freedom to squirm behind the wood paneling, where they died long, wiggling deaths and then slowly decomposed.

Through it all, Schwartzman never once responded to God.

He never prayed, he never beseeched, he never begged. He didn't repent, he didn't give charity, he didn't donate to the synagogue building fund.

He stopped going to synagogue entirely.

He had an Egg McMuffin with bacon and cheese every morning, and mixed his meat dishes with his dairy dishes every night.

And yet, despite all their misfortunes, the loss of every one of their pets, and the loss of every one of the pets they'd bought to replace their original pets, the Schwartzmans had never been happier.

They took long walks on Saturday mornings.

They bought nonkosher pretzels from nonkosher street vendors and covered them with nonkosher mustard.

They went for Saturday afternoon drives to nearby parks and faraway museums.

Instead of watching Leno, they made love.

And behold, one Thursday night later that summer, God spoke to a Mr. Akiva Twersky in Kew Gardens, Queens, saying, "Make for yourself an ark, for you and your entire family, because I have found you righteous in your generation."

"Who's that?" called out the terrified Twersky. "Hello? Who's there? Who's talking?"

Schmuck.

They're All
the Same

A T twelve noon and one one-thousandth of a thousandth of a second, God strode through the front door of the Manhattan advertising offices of Goldsmith Deutsch & McCabe.

His appointment was for twelve.

The morning had begun at a frenetic pace. God was expected and everybody was busily tidying up their workspaces, emptying wastepaper baskets, pulling down on their hemlines and deleting pornography from their hard drives. Goldsmith Deutsch & McCabe had all of God's North American business, and they were keen to add His global business to their roster.

God didn't just walk through the etched smoked glass front door of GDM every day. There were fresh bagels at reception, cut daisies in the women's restroom, and not a single used condom in the men's. Nobody told anyone to fuck off, no one complained about the crappy coffee, no one smacked his computer and loudly proclaimed it a lousy motherfucker.

At roughly five minutes after twelve, Goldsmith came out to meet Him.

Let the bastard wait, thought Goldsmith.

"Hey, God!" Goldsmith called, doing his best to smile, shaking God's hand firmly. "Good to see you. No one told me you were coming in today. How are you doing?"

"Worse now," said God.

Everyone laughed.

Prick, thought Goldsmith.

Deutsch hurried over and quickly wedged himself between Goldsmith and one of the agency's highest-paying clients (Procter & Gamble was number one).

"C'mon! C'mon! Let's go inside. We've got bagels. . . ."

The agency had spent the last six months preparing for this meeting. They ran focus groups in New York, London, Prague and Detroit. Respondents

were separated into three groups: Believers, Nonbelievers and what they had ultimately defined as the
target with the greatest possible potential, Persuad-
ables.

They conducted e-research, consisting of e-polls
and e-surveys, presented in a document titled *e-
Findings* that they had e-published on the Web. Respondents had been asked a number of questions:

1. If God were a person, who would He be?
2. Would you want to work for God? Would you
   want God to work for you?
3. Would you vote for God if He ran for President?
4. God is at a party. Is He (A) the life of the party,
   (B) a wallflower, or (C) drunk and disorderly?
5. God shows up at your doorstep. He is wearing
   (A) shoes, (B) sneakers, or (C) God is barefoot.

They did concept testing of a number of prelimi-
nary taglines and positioning statements. Nobody in
the focus groups liked "The Original and Still the
Best," they were split on "The Porsche of Deities"
and "Feeling Odd? Try God" met with consistent
disapproval. One elderly woman took personal of-

fense with the latter as she understood the tagline to be suggesting that if she believed in God, she must be odd; a meaningful discussion nearly ensued, and an emergency plate of doughnuts was hurried in.

The meeting began. Everyone wore bright, colorful creative-looking ties, the walls were covered with bright colorful ads and the table was covered with bright colorful food.

God took His usual seat at the head of the table.

Figures, thought Goldsmith. If there was one thing that thirty years in the advertising business had taught him, it was that these guys were all the same. Where were the titanium Palm Pilot and Tag Heuer watch?

God took off his Tag Heuer watch and laid it down on the table beside his titanium Palm Pilot.

"Where's McCabe?" asked God. "We should at least have one goy in the room, shouldn't we?"

Everyone laughed.

"He's in the Caribbean," Deutsch said. "Silver wedding anniversary. St. Bart's."

"Ever since *The Simpsons* I just can't go there," joked Goldsmith.

Nobody laughed.

"I'd like to go over the agenda before we get

started," said Stacy, the energetic young account executive. Stacy told them that they would begin with a light breakfast, then a debrief on the rebrief of the last brief, then Research, then TV advertising ideas, then more Research, then Print advertising ideas, then Research again, and then a light lunch.

They would be given a research document on their way out.

Stacy invited them all to the breakfast buffet set up in the corner. Before she could even finish, God jumped up and raced straight for the crullers. Goldsmith tried to pass him at the corner of the table, but God zipped past and grabbed them from the plate. Goldsmith had to settle for a lousy croissant.

Figures, thought Goldsmith.

Goldsmith's mother had passed away just twenty-three days ago after a long and difficult battle with Alzheimer's. God had apologized and expressed his sincerest regrets in an e-mail addressed to the entire agency. "In her memory," he wrote, "we should all redouble our efforts and commitment to this most important project."

Goldsmith didn't care for God's apology. He wasn't angry about his mother's death; death happens. But he was angry about her suffering. He could well understand that there were things he could not understand, but the need for suffering was something he never wanted to understand. He couldn't stomach the sight of God these days, but what was he going to do? Tell the firm's biggest client to go fuck Himself?

Quietly, though, Goldsmith was having his own small revenge. Despite pressure from Deutsch and McCabe, he had refused to give God the CEO commercial that he no doubt wanted.

If there was a second thing that Goldsmith had learned after thirty years in the advertising business, it was that, ultimately, every CEO wants to star in his own commercial. The CEO commercial gave them the chance to do that, disguising their narcissism and vanity as accessibility and concern. From Iacocca to God, they were all the same.

Hello, I'm an egomaniac, and today I'd like to talk to you about me.

Goldsmith wouldn't do it.

He wouldn't give it to Him.

We open on God in a field, making the flowers bloom! We cut to God in a forest, making the birds sing! We cut to God in a hospital, bringing babies into the world!

No fucking way.

"Okay, folks," called Stacy, "let's get started."

Goldsmith was still waiting for God to pull His nose out of the creamer.

"Beautiful day," Goldsmith tried.

"I made it myself," God answered loudly.

Everyone laughed.

STACY turned off the overhead lights and started the projector. God wondered aloud how much of that projector came out of His pocket.

"Seventeen percent commission, my ass," He said. Everyone laughed.

Stacy began.

The harsh reality was this: God was skewing old. And white. Of course, it was a difficult market. His numbers were through the mosque's roof in the East, but in the West, God was in the toilet. As chart A clearly showed, there had been a short spike in His awareness levels immediately following 9/11, but it had been a nearly continuous freefall ever since—and even back then, His awareness was skewing negative.

In response, as charts B, C, D and E showed, the agency had conducted focus groups in Atlanta, Houston and Chicago. They had given a roomful of college-educated men and women aged twenty-one to thirty-five earning over $50,000 per year a deck of picture cards. On each card was a picture of a famous celebrity, along with one extra card that just read "God." There were two white boards hung on the wall; one board was labeled "Cool," the other was labeled "Not Cool." The moderators directed them to pin their celebrities to whichever board they felt most accurately described them.

Jon Stewart, Quentin Tarantino and Moby all made it to the Cool board; Colin Powell and Rob Lowe did not.

Most worrisome, Stacy concluded, was that in the opinion of sixty-eight college-educated men and women aged twenty-one to thirty-five and making over $50,000 a year, God was definitely "not cool."

God was right up there between Carrot Top and Gallagher.

The projector was turned off, the lights were turned on and Goldsmith stood up. Presenting the ad campaign was his part of the show.

He picked up his presentation boards and carried them to the head of the table.

He tried to put aside his personal feelings toward God. He was a professional, after all, and this meeting was the culmination of six long months of work. Six months of early mornings and late nights, six months of Start Dinner Without Me and Not This Weekend, Mom, I'm Working.

"We have been working long and hard on this campaign," Goldsmith began.

God was rudely writing on his titanium Palm Pilot.

"Kick puppy," Goldsmith imagined.

Goldsmith's mother hated those Palm Pilot things. He'd bought her one for what turned out to be her last birthday in an attempt to cheer her up. But her hands shook too much and she couldn't remember the strange new alphabet. She liked to hold it, though; Goldsmith liked to imagine it reminded her of him. More likely, she just thought it was a Bible.

God smacked his Palm Pilot angrily and threw it onto the table. "Piece of shit," he said loudly.

Deutsch smiled and tried to direct God's attention toward Goldsmith.

"We want your business," continued Goldsmith, "not just for the revenue, but because we truly want you to succeed."

He loathed himself. He loathed every last cell in his body.

God was still grumbling about the Palm Pilot.

"Why is every fucking thing those fucking Japs make such a piece of shit? Why?"

Everyone laughed.

"We're going to show you a range of ideas," Goldsmith soldiered on, "and I want to emphasize that these are just ideas, just works in progress."

"You mean they suck?" God quipped. "What are you, a fucking Jap now?"

Everyone laughed.

Even Goldsmith laughed.

Goldsmith laughed and laughed, long after everyone else had stopped. "Everything's funny when you're paying the bills," Goldsmith laughed, and then he laughed some more.

"I'm not paying *your* bills," God said coldly.

Everyone laughed.

If there was a third thing that Goldsmith had learned after thirty years in the advertising business it was that sometimes, with some clients, "fuck you" is a valid answer.

"Fuck you," Goldsmith said.

Nobody laughed.

•••

THE account was eventually awarded to Ogilvy and Mather. The contact report made no mention of the incident. "Client was appreciative of the effort the agency clearly made on His behalf, but Client wondered if the Client's needs demanded an agency of a more established nature."

Everyone at GDM agreed that God would have made a terrible client. Very P&G.

Procter & Gamble. A notoriously difficult client.

"Let's just focus on the Nike pitch," said Deutsch.

A few days later, Goldsmith called the team into his office. A producer in L.A. owed him a favor and he held in his hand the Ogilvy rough cut of God's new commercial.

We open on God in a field, He's making the flowers bloom! We cut to God in a forest, making the birds sing! We cut to God in a hospital, bringing babies into the world!

They're all the same.

Smite the Heathens, Charlie Brown

CHARLIE BROWN, walking down the street. He is wearing his baseball cap and is smiling.

He meets Linus.

Charlie Brown says: There's something magical about the very first baseball game of the season.

Linus says, "Schulz died last night."

"Good grief," says Charlie Brown.

LINUS and Charlie Brown, walking down the street.

Linus says, "Last night someone spray-painted a giant pumpkin on our front door."

Linus says, "This morning I prayed to the Great Pumpkin to protect us from the rioting Schulzians."

Charlie Brown asks, "How's Lucy taking it?"

Lucy strolls over.

"NEVER AGAIN!" she shouts, flipping the boys upside down.

Linus says, "Personally."

CHARLIE BROWN, sitting in his beanbag chair. He is watching TV. Sally stands behind him.

Sally asks, "Are we Schulzian or Pumpkinite?"

Charlie Brown says, "We're Schulzian."

Charlie Brown says, "Schulzians believe in a Creator who writes and draws us every single day . . ."

Charlie Brown says, ". . . while Pumpkinites, like Linus and Lucy, believe in the Great Pumpkin who flies around and rewards his believers on Halloween."

Charlie Brown says, "But ultimately, belief should be a personal choice."

"Which one gets more vacation?" asks Sally.

Charlie Brown rolls his eyes.

CHARLIE BROWN and Linus, standing behind the old stone wall.

Linus ducks.

Snoopy and Woodstock stroll over. Snoopy wears a beret and carries a rifle on his shoulder. Snoopy's shirt reads: SCHULZ IS THE LORD.

Snoopy and Woodstock leave.

Linus stands up.

"Good grief," says Charlie Brown.

SNOOPY sits on the roof of his doghouse, facing his typewriter. Woodstock sits on Snoopy's shoulder.

Charlie Brown strolls over.

Snoopy hands him a page.

Charlie Brown reads: "The only final solution is to kill all the Pumpkinites as they have killed Schulz our Lord."

Charlie Brown looks up at Snoopy.

"Mein Kampf," says Snoopy.

Woodstock starts shouting loudly and waving his red pen.

"Mein editor," says Snoopy.

SNOOPY sits on the roof of his doghouse, facing his typewriter.

Snoopy types: "It was a dark and stormy night."

Snoopy thinks.

Snoopy thinks.

Snoopy thinks.

Snoopy writes: "Because of the lousy Pumpkinites."

Snoopy smiles.

LUCY holds the football for Charlie Brown.

Lucy says, "There's so much hatred and animosity in this world."

Charlie Brown runs toward the football.

Lucy says: "Maybe one day, in some distant utopian future, we can stop this hideous cycle of violence once and for all."

Lucy pulls the ball away and Charlie Brown falls flat on his back.

"That's a beautiful sentiment," says Charlie Brown.

"I'm a beautiful person," says Lucy.

LUCY leans against Schroeder's piano as Schroeder plays.

Lucy says, "Before we get married, you should know that I don't believe in Schulz. I'm devoutly Pumpkinite."

Schroeder says, "I don't believe in either Schulz or the Great Pumpkin. I believe that our purpose on Earth is an inner journey of exploration and honesty not an outward journey of conquest and domination."

Schroeder goes back to playing his piano.

Lucy says, "I don't believe in Schulz, either."

Schroeder rolls his eyes.

CHARLIE BROWN and Linus, standing behind the old stone wall.

Charlie Brown says, "My religion is baseball. My church is the pitcher's mound."

Charlie Brown says, "The moment a team steps onto that mystical field, all differences between them are forgotten. It is no small miracle but that for one small moment, nine different people become as one."

Snoopy strolls over to Linus. He is carrying a baseball bat over his shoulder.

Snoopy smashes Linus in the head.

Charlie Brown says, "Good grief."

CHARLIE BROWN, standing outside Snoopy's jail cell.

Snoopy says, "On the contrary—I plead guilty!"

Snoopy says, "I am a soldier in the army of Schulz, and I shall proudly smite the nonbeliever wherever he may be."

Charlie Brown says, "If you plead not guilty we can be home in time for dinner."

Snoopy's ears stand straight up.

Charlie Brown and Snoopy, walking home. Snoopy thinks: Even zealots get the munchies.

LUCY and Linus, walking down the street. Linus's head is wrapped in a bandage.

They meet Charlie Brown and Snoopy.

Lucy says, "We refuse to play on a baseball team with Snoopy."

Snoopy says, "I refuse to play on a baseball team with them."

Nobody says anything.

Charlie Brown says, "Hatred is something everyone can agree on."

CHARLIE BROWN, slumped down in his beanbag chair. He is watching TV. Sally stands behind him.

Charlie Brown says, "I give up. Maybe we should all just stay apart. Maybe we should all just build our walls and fences and defend them night and day with our barbed wire and guard dogs. Why should I be the only one who cares? So what if I never see or speak to another Pumpkinite for the rest of my life? What do I care?"

Sally asks, "All the Pumpkinites?"

Charlie Brown says, "All the Pumpkinites."

"Even the Little Red Haired Pumpkinites?" asks Sally.

"Aauugghh!" screams Charlie Brown.

CHARLIE BROWN, walking across the lawn.

He meets Snoopy, who carries a rifle over his shoulder and wears a T-shirt that reads WHAT WOULD SCHULZ DO?

Behind him, a small group of Woodstocks stand in precise military formation.

Snoopy says, "Snoopy Youth."

"Good grief," says Charlie Brown.

CHARLIE BROWN strolls over to Lucy. She is wearing a beret and a T-shirt that reads P.D.L.

They look at each other.

They look at each other.

They look at each other.

Lucy says, "Pumpkinish Defense League."

Charlie Brown rolls his eyes.

CHARLIE BROWN, standing on the pitcher's mound. It is pouring rain.

"Good grief," says Charlie Brown.

Charlie Brown pitches and asks, "What are you called when you're not sure who the Creator is . . ."

POW! The ball is hit so hard that it flips Charlie Brown upside down.

He lands flat on his back.

". . . but you're pretty sure that He hates you?"

Linus strolls over.

"A Chucknostic," he says.

CHARLIE BROWN, standing on the pitcher's mound. It is pouring rain.

He watches the ball as it sails over his head.

He watches the ball as it flies to the outfield.

Lucy, standing in the outfield wearing her baseball hat and her P.D.L. T-shirt. She holds a tall black flag with a large orange pumpkin on it.

"Never forget, Charlie Brown!" shouts Lucy.

The ball drops right beside her.

"Good grief," says Charlie Brown.

SNOOPY, at bat. It is pouring rain.

Snoopy thinks: Everyone knows the Pumpkins are behind Schulz's death! Pumpkins are behind everything. Their secret international organization covertly influences and informs every single. . . .

The pitch goes whizzing past.

Snoopy swings and misses.

"Strike!" calls the umpire.

Snoopy walks angrily back to the bench.

Snoopy thinks: Sneaky Pumpkinites.

CHARLIE BROWN, standing on the pitcher's mound. It is pouring rain.

Charlie Brown pitches the ball.

There is a loud POW! as someone hits a homer that flips Charlie Brown upside down and knocks him out of his shoes.

Charlie Brown lands on his back atop the pitcher's mound.

Linus approaches from second base and Schroeder approaches from home plate.

Linus says, "Can you believe those lousy Schulzians are going to beat us, Charlie Brown?"

Schroeder says, "I'll tell you what I believe. I believe in Man. I believe in feeling and music and art. I believe that we are all individual parts of one larger God, and that by serving one another we will ultimately be serving ourselves."

Schroeder walks away.

"FAG!" shouts Linus.

SNOOPY, at bat. It is pouring rain.

CRACK! as he hits the ball.

Lucy runs for the ball.

Snoopy runs for the base.

Lucy runs for the ball.

Snoopy runs for the base.

CRASH! as Lucy and Snoopy violently collide. They point at one another and shout: "NAZI!"

CHARLIE BROWN is slumped down in his beanbag chair, watching television. Sally stands behind him.

The television announcer says, "Yesterday's collision between Snoopy and Lucy only increased tension between the rival religious sects."

Charlie Brown says, "Some people say that sports are nothing more than a tool of the government to distract us from the pain of our miserable lives."

The television announcer says, "The National Guard has been deployed as widespread rioting continues across town."

"Wanna have a catch?" asks Sally.

Charlie Brown and Sally run out the door.

LUCY sits glumly on her couch, her foot in a cast.

Snoopy lies glumly on his doghouse, his nose in a splint.

Linus sits glumly in his security blanket, his head wrapped in a bandage.

Charlie Brown stands glumly behind the old stone wall.

Nobody strolls over.

Nobody strolls over.

Nobody strolls over.

"Good grief," says Charlie Brown.

God Is a Big
Happy Chicken

WHEN Yankel Morgenstern died and went to heaven, he was surprised to discover that God was a large chicken. The chicken was around thirty feet tall, and spoke perfect English. He stood before a gleaming eternal coop of gold made of chicken wire of shimmering bronze, and behold, inside, a nest of diamonds.

"Fuck," said Morgenstern.

"You know," said Chicken, "that's the first thing everyone says when they meet me. " 'Fuck.' How does that make me feel?"

Morgenstern threw himself at Chicken's feet, kissing his enormous holy claws.

"Hear O Israel, the Lord is your God, the Lord is One!" Morgenstern cried out.

Chicken stepped backward and shrugged.

"Eh?" he said, bobbing his enormous head.

"What?" asked Morgenstern.

"What's that supposed to do for me? Hero Israel . . . ?" he asked. "How's it go again?" asked Chicken.

"It's . . . it's Shema," Morgenstern said with hesitation.

Chicken stomped around in a circle before settling down in His Holy Nest of Nests. "Yeah," he said. "I know. I've been hearing it for years. Still not sure what it means, though. Hero Israel—"

"Not hero Israel," snapped Morgenstern. He stood up, clutching his black felt hat in his hand. "Hear, O Israel. It means that you are one, that you are the only, you know . . . God."

That last word didn't come easily.

"Of course I am," said Chicken. "Do you see any other Chickens around here?"

Morgenstern thought of his wife and children down on Earth, praying uselessly to a nonfowl deity that didn't exist. He thought of all the chickens he'd eaten. Breasts, thighs, giblets, nuggets. So many omelets. Western. Spanish. Californian. Dear God. It was true that in the few months before his death he had switched to free-range, but would that earn the Chicken's mercy? He thought of the fast-food industry, of KFC, of the horrible retribution spicy chicken wings would surely bring upon all mankind.

"Hey Gabe! Gabe!" called the Chicken. "Is it Hero Israel, or Hear O Israel?"

A stocky old man appeared from the clouds. He wore a pair of dirty Carhartt overalls and smoked a cigarette.

"It is Hero Israel, Sir. You are quite correct." He turned his head sharply toward Morgenstern.

"Morgenstern?"

"Yes?"

"Follow me."

Morgenstern bowed to the large chicken and walked backward from Him in a show of deference and respect, but when he looked up, Chicken was already beak-deep in His golden bowl of feed.

Morgenstern felt dizzy. This was all too much.

"Was that really . . . ?"

Gabe nodded.

"But the Bible—" said Morgenstern.

"Don't you worry about the Bible," said Gabe. "We've got the joker who wrote that thing down in hell. Gabe," he said, extending his hand to Morgenstern as they walked through the Nothingness toward the Nowhere.

"As in Gabriel, right?" asked Morgenstern. "I expected you to be more, I don't know—"

"Jewish?"

"I suppose," answered Morgenstern.

"Asians all think I'd be Asian. Black folks all think I'd be black. It's a funny world. I'm sort of the head ranch hand around here. I make sure Chicken has enough feed and water, I clean his coop. You know, general maintenance."

"Couldn't The Chicken just create his own food?"

"Not 'The Chicken,' just 'Chicken.' And no, he can't create his own food. He's a chicken."

Morgenstern asked Gabe where he was taking him.

"Nowhere. This is what we do here. Wherever you go, there you are."

"Christ," cried Morgenstern. "You're Buddhist! I

knew it. God is a Buddhist! Damn damn damn! I knew the Buddhists were right. Always so happy and peaceful."

"He's not a Buddhist," interrupted Gabe. He paused to light a cigarette. Marlboro, Reds. "He's a chicken."

"I need to go back to Earth," Morgenstern blurted out.

"Earth? Why?"

Morgenstern turned to face Gabe.

"Let me tell them, Gabe. Please. Let me tell my family, just my family, Gabe. He's a chicken! Not Hashem, Not Adonai! Oh, the years I wasted! Let me tell them so they don't have to jump through the hoops I did, trying to please some maniacal father who art in heaven! Nine children, Gabe. Nine full, happy, worry-free lives! Let them drive on Saturday, let them eat bacon, let them get the lunch special at Red Lobster! McDonald's, Gabe! Do you have any of those fries up here, do you? What does a hamburger with cheese taste like? Is anal sex all it's cracked up to be? Please, Gabe! They can have abs. They can drive Camaros. They can watch television on Friday night. I never saw an episode of *Miami Vice*, Gabe, never. Mine was no life. I was raised like a veal. Not chosen.

Just . . . people. Oh, what freedom. Please. Let me tell them, Gabe."

Gabe took a long drag from his cigarette and shook his head.

"They won't listen," he said. "I've tried telling a few myself. But you want to go back to Earth? Go. Go back to Earth."

Morgenstern hugged Gabe tightly.

"Don't you have to clear it with The Chicken?"

"Not 'The Chicken,' " said Gabe, "just 'Chicken.' And no, I don't. Chicken doesn't care either way." He flicked his cigarette butt off to the side. "He gets his feed filled in the morning, and his droppings cleaned in the afternoon and that's all He really wants to know. I'll see ya in a couple years."

"Hey!" a voice from below called upward. "Watch where you flick your butts!"

"Well, well!" Gabe shouted down. "If it isn't Mr. Bible Writer."

"I said I was sorry!" the man shouted back.

When Gabe looked up, Morgenstern was gone.

MORGENSTERN awoke. He rolled his head slowly to the side and saw his wife and his daughter Hannah sitting at the table in the hospital room, eating their dinner.

Chicken.

"Don't . . . eat. . . ." was all he could manage.

His wife jumped, startled at his sudden awakening.

"Boruch Hashem!" she clapped. "Blessed is the Lord who makes miracles happen every day! Don't shake your head, Yankel, you have tubes in your nose. Hannah, come quick, your father is alive!"

His daughter approached cautiously, holding a bar-becued chicken drumstick in her right hand and a half-eaten wing in her left.

"May Hashem grant you a full and speedy recov-ery," she mumbled in Yiddish while staring at her shoes. She spotted a piece of barbecued God on her blouse, picked it off with her greasy little fingers and popped it into her mouth.

Morgenstern groaned and passed out.

FRIDAY afternoon he was back home in his very own bed. He'd decided to put off telling his family about Chicken until he was out of the hospital. He would tell them tonight, as they gathered around the Shabbos table. He would speak to them the

Word of Chicken, and thus would they be freed.

Maybe jump in the car afterward, catch a movie.

When the sun had finally set and Shabbos had finally arrived, Morgenstern pulled himself into his wheelchair, took a deep breath and rolled himself into the dining room.

His wife had set the table with the good tablecloth, the good silverware and the good glasses. He watched her light the good Shabbos candles, covering her face with her hands and silently praying to a God who wasn't there.

"Please hear my blessings," she prayed to nobody, "in the merit of Sarah, Rebecca, Rachel and Leah."

She'd have had better luck with a handful of scratch. Maybe some cut-up apple.

She turned to him with love in her eyes.

"Blessed is God," she said in Yiddish.

She came to him, knelt beside his wheelchair and hugged him.

"I have to tell you something," he said.

"I know," she sobbed into the good napkin. "I know."

"I don't think you do."

He rolled away from her. "When I was dead," said Morgenstern, "I met God."

"We all meet God every day," said his wife, "if only you know where to look."

"No!" shouted Morgenstern. "You're not listening! How do you think I got back here?" he asked her.

"Who else but the All-Merciful would send you back to me?"

He could take no more.

"Who?" shouted Morgenstern as he wheeled himself around to the head of the table. "I'll tell you who!"

The loud voices attracted the children, and they gathered slowly around the Shabbos table.

"Let me tell you a little something about your, uh, All-Knowing! Let me tell you a little something about your All-Merciful!"

Morgenstern looked from Shmuel to Yonah to Meyer to Rivka to Dovid to Hannah to Deena to Leah to little Yichezkel.

The children were all showered, their hair neatly combed, and dressed in their finest Shabbos clothes.

He looked at his wife. She was wearing his favorite wig. There was a picture of Jerusalem on the wall above her right shoulder, some family pictures above her left. Bar mitzvahs, weddings, last year's seder at the Fontainebleau Hotel in Miami.

"Children," he began.

"God," he said.

"Is," he continued.

"A," he added.

The light from the Shabbos candles flickered in the eyes of his children. Little Meyer was wearing a brand new yarmulke, and couldn't stop fidgeting with it. Shmuel held a handful of Torah notes from his rabbi he would read after the meal, and the girls would be looking forward to singing their favorite Shabbos songs.

"God is a what?" asked little Hannah.

He couldn't do it.

"God," Morgenstern said to his children, "is a merciful God." His wife came to his side. "He is the God of our forefathers. Blessed is God who in His mercy restores life to the dead."

The children cheered.

"Amen, may His name be called out in joy!" they shouted, jumping up from their seats to hug him all at once.

Morgenstern closed his eyes and hugged his children tightly.

His wife bent over and kissed him gently on his

forehead. "May His kindness shine down on us forever," she whispered.

She smiled then, went into the kitchen and
brought out the soup.

Chicken.

It Ain't Easy
Bein' Supremey

*C*OME! *Let us now sing out to Epstein!*
Let us call out in praise to the Rock of Salvation!
Let me greet him with thanksgiving, with praiseful songs let me pray to him.
For a great God is Epstein, and a great King above all!

While it is true that the latest edition of *Kabbalah For Dummies* is an engaging and often thought-provoking introduction to the concepts of that renowned work of ancient Jewish mysticism, it might have been prudent if somewhere in the "Golem" section, perhaps adjacent to the detailed instructions on how to create one, they might have mentioned, however cursorily, how to uncreate one.

For I am not but a mound of dirt, of clay, of earth, into which Epstein in His great mercy did breathe life. Command me, Epstein, and I shall obey. Let me now praise Epstein, Amen.

"Holy crap," said Epstein, "it worked."

Epstein's mother clapped her hands excitedly. "Ooo, make him do something, Moshe! Make him do something!"

The golem sat upright on Epstein's couch, his back straight, his hands clasped solemnly in front of his chest. Epstein had dressed him in one of his old blue business suits, with a wide striped tie and a dark gray fedora. He wasn't beautiful, or even symmetrical, but for a first Golem, he was pretty damn good.

"Behold!" said Epstein. "I command you to, uh, stand up!"

The golem stood up.

The Epsteins gasped.

"Behold!" said Epstein. "I command you to sit!"

And the golem sat.

Epstein's mother cheered. "Can I try, can I try?"

She thought for a moment.

"Behold!" she suddenly called out. "Do the laundry!"

The Epsteins held their breath.

"Hanging or folded?" the golem asked.

Epstein's mother squealed.

THIS is the life," said Epstein.

The plants were watered, the cat was fed and the garbage had already been taken out. Sunday afternoon, nothing to do but sit back with a cold beer and watch the Jets game with his mother.

"Golem!" Epstein called out.

"Here I am," said the golem.

"Bring unto me a beer," said Epstein, "and with it some of those chips. You know, in the tall cupboard by the stove."

He was sure getting to like that golem.

"Hark," cried out the golem, "dost thou desire a Beck's or dost Thou desire a Samuel Adams?"

"I desire," called out Epstein, "a Samuel Adams."

"Amen," said the golem. "Light or Regular?"

"Regular."

"Ale or lager?"

"Lager."

"Amber or Cherry Wheat?"

"Just get me a fucking beer," said Epstein.

And the golem hurried out.

Sweet.

"What a nice boy," said Epstein's mother.

A moment later, the golem returned.

"Barbecue chips or Zesty Ranch?" he asked.

Epstein is my shepherd, I shall not lack. In lush meadows He lays me down, beside tranquil waters He leads me. I shall dwell in the house of Epstein for all of my days.

Epstein was thirty-seven years old, a low-level assistant in an insignificant branch of a monolithic corporation with offices in seventy-two countries including Bahrain. He was a cog in the wheel of another wheel with cogs of its own. His devoted golem may have known him as Epstein the All-Powerful and Omniscient, but most everyone else knew him as Epstein the Balding Junior Assistant to the Fat Guy in Accounting with the Lisp. And while yes, it may have been factually true that he lived with his mother, technically speaking his mother lived with him, a semantic loophole which never failed to fail to impress the ladies.

He couldn't just throw her out on the street. She was old and needed his company, and he was young and needed her half of the rent.

But goddamn it, it was high time someone took care of Epstein for a change! It was time someone wanted Epstein's opinion, time someone brought Epstein a coffee.

Morning, Mr. Epstein!

Whatever you say, Mr. Epstein!

But what do *you* think, Mr. Epstein?

Last Saturday afternoon, as part of his weekly sermon, Rabbi Teitelbaum told the congregation the story of the Golem of Prague; by Saturday night, Epstein was already scouring the Golem section in the local Barnes & Noble (it's not in Sci-Fi, by the way, it's in Biography). One quick stop at Home Depot for a half-dozen bags of dirt, and Epstein was set.

Epstein raised me from the pit of raging waters, from the slimy mud did he lift me. Praiseworthy is he who places in Epstein his trust, who turns not to the strayers after falsehood.

Epstein was starting to like all this Thou Thee Thy Beseech stuff. Nobody beseeched him at work. Nobody praised him. Nobody sanctified his name. Most of them didn't even remember his name.

The golem was a real bower, which Epstein liked—he bowed when he entered the room, he bowed when he left, he bowed when he began to speak and he bowed when he stopped—and he never once forgot his Morning Praise, a short hymn Epstein composed called *Obey Me or Else*:

Blessed is He that broughteth you into this world, for He can surely taketh you out.

That Epstein had no idea how to kill a golem, considering that they weren't technically alive, didn't trouble him too deeply.

And so, two weeks and a couple of trips back to the Home Depot Garden Center later, Epstein was back in the garden, busily creating Golem Two.

Epstein had discovered the first time around that despite what *Kabbalah For Dummies* said, creation was really more of a two-man job. Sure, you might be able to pull it off by yourself; others famously had, of course, but they had obviously cut corners. To begin with, the bags of dirt were heavy—fifty pounds each of the appropriately named Miracle-Gro Garden

Soil—and you needed at least a dozen of them for a Golem of even modest size. Then you had to shape the dirt into something resembling a man, which sounds a lot easier than it is, particularly if you're going for the whole in-your-own-image thing (which *Kabbalah For Dummies* advised against while still acknowledging that "it is kinda the fun part").

Golem One had turned out well enough, and even looked a little like Epstein—medium height, bit of a gut. That must have been beginner's luck, though, because Epstein was having a hell of a time with the legs on Golem Two, and he kept screwing up the head.

He wasn't very good at heads.

"Come on, Ma!" called Epstein. "I need a hand with this one!"

He found her downstairs in the laundry room, an angry scowl on her face, her foot tapping impatiently on the laundry room floor where a tall pile of laundry sat silently stinking. The golem was bent over the dryer, writing notes in yet another of his thick black notebooks. He carried those notebooks everywhere, recording in great detail every Epsteinian rule and regulation. In the few short weeks since his creation, he'd filled seven of them from cover to cover. There was an entire volume on beer, and two on the complex subject of chips and related snacks. Another tractate covered all the laws of housecleaning, while still another catechized the full care and feeding of house plants and window boxes (container plants demanded a volume all their own).

When he wasn't writing in them, he was consulting from them.

The covers were already worn, the pages already weathered and loose.

"Hark," cried out the golem, "when Thou say detergent, art thou referring to powdered detergent or to liquid detergent?"

"Liquid," snapped Epstein's mother.

The golem wrote that down.

"How about those detergent disks?" he asked.

"We don't have detergent disks."

"Shall I get detergent disks?"

"Liquid is fine."

"Tide or Wisk?"

"Tide."

"What about Fab?"

"No."

"Gain?"

Epstein's mother shook her head.

"Tide with Bleach Alternative or Tide with Bleach Ultra?"

"We don't have Tide with Bleach Ultra."

"Shall I get Tide with Bleach Ultra?"

She groaned.

"What the hell's wrong with him, Moshe?"

"Give him some time," said Epstein.

"To him, time must be given," said the golem, turning to a blank page in his notebook. "Now then—lay flat or tumble dry?"

Mrs. Epstein slammed the washer shut and stormed out of the room.

"Delicate or permanent press?" the golem called out after her. He ran to the doorway, clutching his precious notebook to his chest.

"Delicate or permanent press!"

This I will know, that Epstein is with me. When Epstein acts in strict justice, I still praise the Word. When Epstein acts in mercy, I still praise the Word. In Epstein I have trusted, I shall not fear.

"This place is a wreck," said Epstein's mother.

It had been two weeks since Golem Two's creation, and well over a month since Golem One's.

The plants hadn't been watered, the cat hadn't been fed and the garbage hadn't been taken out.

Neither golem was doing very much at all these days, stuck as they were in near constant debate about the meaning, intricacies and inferences of Epstein's instructions and commands.

"Epstein clearly said to separate whites and colors," said Golem One.

"I don't disagree with that," said Golem Two. "I disagree with how you interpret the word 'colors.' You hold that any amount of color constitutes color, whereas I hold that it has to be a significant amount of color."

The pile of soiled clothing in the center of the laundry room had already doubled in size. Dirty linens were piled high in the sink, underwear hung from every doorknob and light switch, and Epstein's mother's beige underwire bras were slung sloppily over the top of the laundry room door.

"But what is a 'significant' amount of color?" asked Golem One.

Golem Two cited Notebook 4, page 42 of Epstein's Laws concerning the taking out the garbage, wherein the garbage being "significantly" full meant that the lid could not be closed. According to Golem Two, significant therefore meant a majority of or a predominance of. Golem One argued that garbage was a different ruling entirely because it depended on the day of the week—that is, the *time* the garbage was picked up—not on an *amount* of garbage, as was the issue in the case of the dirty laundry.

Epstein separated the whites from the colors himself, filled the washing machine, slammed the door and left.

The golems fell to their knees and begged for forgiveness:

Behold, before you I am like a vessel filled with shame and humiliation! May it be your will, O Epstein, that I not sin again!

And then, one Sunday afternoon, after watering the plants, feeding the cat and taking out the garbage, Epstein barely had enough time to sit back without his cold beer and catch the last lousy couple of minutes of the Jets game with his mother.

When the golems came and joined them in the den, Epstein's mother left without a word.

"No!" Epstein shouted at the television. "Go for the field goal!"

"Yes, yes," agreed Golem One. "The field goal is what they should go for."

"We should all go for the field goal," Golem Two concurred.

"By going for the field goal," added Golem One, "we all will be rewarded."

It was third and long, with less than two minutes to play and the Jets were only down by one.

"You never pass on third and long," said Epstein.

"Passing on third and long is wrong," said Golem Two.

"He who passes on third and long," said Golem One, "shall surely be put to death."

The quarterback dropped back, faked left, reared back and threw the ball into the end zone.

"It's up . . . !" said Epstein. "Touchdown!" he shouted, jumping out of his seat. "Woo! In your face!"

Epstein raised his arms above his head and turned for the double high-five to the golems, who remained sitting, as ever, solemnly in their seats.

"Touchdown," nodded Golem One sagely.

"Amen," agreed Golem Two, scribbling away in his notebook. "In their face."

•••

RABBI Teitelbaum peeked through his living room window, and unlocked the front door.

"Epstein!" he said. "How's your mother?"

The Rabbi led Epstein into his study, and closed the door.

"I have a problem," said Epstein.

"Yes, yes," said Rabbi Teitelbaum. He stood by the window, looking out at his cars in the driveway and stroking his long, silvery beard. After some polite small talk about the situation in Israel and the paltry synagogue building fund, Epstein confessed that despite the repeated cautions, he had kinda sorta made himself a golem.

"Two, actually. It seemed like a good idea at the time. I'm just so busy, you know, with Mother, and, well, life these days."

"Yes, yes," said Rabbi Teitelbaum. "With the multitasking and the e-mails, yes, yes." He seemed to be keeping a keen eye on his cars in the driveway.

Epstein continued. The golems had become a serious bother. He felt awful saying so, what with being their creator and all, but didn't Nobel regret creating dynamite? Didn't Einstein regret creating the bomb? And so he had decided to be rid of them, which, much like the creation part, was turning out to be more difficult than it sounded. He'd gone to the library, he'd checked the Internet, but he could not find any information, anywhere, about how to undo what he had so regrettably, short-sightedly, foolishly done. Twice.

Rabbi Teitelbaum nodded sagely.

"Yes, yes," said Rabbi Teitelbaum. "The Google knows many things." He stepped away from the window, and sat down behind his desk.

"Unfortunately," he said, "I can't help you."

There was a knock at the door.

"You see," said Rabbi Teitelbaum, leaning forward as his voice dropped to a whisper, "I've kinda sorta got a little golem problem of my own."

The door opened and a golem walked in. He looked different, this golem; looked a lot, in fact, like Rabbi Teitelbaum—tall and thin, lanky, with a noticeable stoop to his back. Epstein thought the rabbi may have been a bit generous with the clay in the crotch area, but overall, it was an impressive effort.

"Nice job," said Epstein.

"Teitelbaum is my shepherd," cried out the golem, *"I shall not lack. In lush meadows He lays me down, beside tranquil waters He leads me."*

Rabbi Teitelbaum shrugged. "It seemed like a

good idea at the time," he said. "That 'crying out' thing gets old fast, doesn't it?"

"Hark," cried out the golem, "when thou say to change the oil in thy car, are thou referring to the minivan or to the sedan?"

The rabbi shook his head.

"The sedan."

"Amen," said the golem. "Regular or synthetic?"

"Regular."

"10W40 or 10W30?"

Rabbi Teitelbaum sighed.

"Just change the fucking oil."

WHEN Epstein returned from the rabbi's house, his mother was waiting for him at the end of their driveway.

"They're killing each other!" she screamed.

The house was a wreck. The dining room table had been flipped over, and two of the wooden chairs had been smashed. In the living room, the couch cushions were torn open and the glass coffee table had been shattered.

"What the hell?" asked Epstein.

"They were arguing!" said Epstein's mother.

Loud shouts and slaps came from the den. Glass shattered.

"Not the television!" cried Epstein.

They ran through the house. The kitchen had been trashed, the cutlery drawer was pulled open and knives were scattered all over the floor. But it was nothing compared to what they found waiting for them in the den.

"Oh my God," said Epstein's mother.

Golem One looked up. "Oh your *what*?"

Golem One was lying on the floor in front of the couch, trying to reach for his legs, both of which had been cut off at the hip, evidently by Golem Two. His right leg was slung over the arm of the far side of the couch, and his left leg was halfway across the room, underneath an overturned end table.

Golem Two wasn't faring much better. He was lying flat on his back in the middle of the room, trying to get to his arms, both of which had been cut off at the shoulder, evidently by Golem One. His right arm was lying at Epstein's feet, his left arm was across the room, sticking out from behind the television.

"He clearly meant to water the plants every day!" Golem Two said loudly to Golem One.

"I don't disagree with that," Golem One answered loudly back, throwing a copy of *TV Guide* at Golem Two's head. "I disagree with your understanding of 'plants' to mean all plants, even those which may not need watering every day, such as the ivy or the little cactus on the window ledge in the kitchen."

Not that it mattered, of course.

The plants had all died weeks ago.

THE golems needed constant supervision.

Golem Two, having no arms, needed Epstein to wash him, clothe him and feed him. If Golem Two wanted a Coke, Epstein not only had to get it for him, Epstein had to hold it for him while he drank.

Golem One, having no legs, needed to be carried to the toilet, and carried off the toilet, and carried to the dinner table and carried to the den to watch TV.

"Epstein!" Golem Two would call out.

"Hark," Epstein would answer.

"Have mercy upon your servant," he would say, "and bring unto me a beer."

"And some chips," added Golem One. "In thy mercy."

So a few weeks later, Epstein awoke in the middle

of the night, helped his mother into the car, and threw their bags into the trunk.

"Fuck this," proclaimed Epstein, and away they went.

OVER the next few weeks, the golems called out for Epstein every morning, every afternoon and every evening, but Epstein did not respond.

Golem One wrote notes on small pieces of paper begging Epstein for forgiveness and salvation, and stuck them in the cracks between the bricks in the living room wall.

Golem Two found a prayer book for Yom Kippur, beat himself on the chest and prayed:

How long, Epstein, will you continue to forget us? How long will you hide your Countenance from us?

The last of the plants withered and died. The cat starved. And the garbage piled high on the living room floor.

About the Author

SHALOM AUSLANDER has written for *Esquire* and *Maxim* and has appeared on NPR's *This American Life*. *Beware of God* was chosen as a finalist for the 2004 Koret Young Writers Award. Shalom lives in Brooklyn.